IN FRANKLIN'S CHAIR

PRIVATE CONVERSATIONS

IN FRANKLIN'S CHAIR
PRIVATE CONVERSATIONS

by

Maggy Clifton

She is wedded to convictions -- in default of grosser ties;
Her contentions are her children, Heaven help him who denies! --
He will meet no suave discussion, but the instant, white-hot, wild,
Wakened female of the species warring as for spouse and child.

Unprovoked and awful charges -- even so the she-bear fights,
Speech that drips, corrodes, and poisons -- even so the cobra bites,
Scientific vivisection of one nerve till it is raw
And the victim writhes in anguish -- like the Jesuit with the squaw!

So it comes that Man, the coward, when he gathers to confer
With his fellow-braves in council, dare not leave a place for her
Where, at war with Life and Conscience, he uplifts his erring hands
To some God of Abstract Justice -- which no woman understands.

And Man knows it! Knows, moreover, that the Woman that God gave
him
Must command but may not govern -- shall enthral but not enslave
him.
And She knows, because She warns him, and Her instincts never fail,
That the Female of Her Species is more deadly than the Male.

—Rudyard Kipling, "Female of the Species," 1911

Contents

Foreword

Writing this collection of humorous…what can I call them? Short stories, perhaps? Anyway, this collection of my observances of the world was something I never thought I could or would ever do. I always thought of myself as a doom-and-gloom writer when it came to writing fiction, not one who could take touchy topics and showcase the absurdities that have increasingly occurred, or rather the absurdities I now recognize as such now that I'm older and I have wisdom by the pound.

I should backtrack a bit, because I'm implying that I miraculously conceived of the idea one glorious morning during one of my many introspective moments, which isn't the case. In fact, the seed for this book was planted in 2009 as I struggled to come up with material for my graduate thesis, a mixed genre collection with a central theme.

The original manuscript I had intended to develop throughout my two years of a Master of Fine Arts (MFA) program, a murder mystery, was obliterated by my writer mentors in the first year; I no longer recognized the work as my own and I decided to shelve it. The problem was I didn't have anything to replace it, which put me in jeopardy of not graduating on time. Attending another semester wasn't an option for me; I had taken out student loans and didn't want to borrow anymore. Besides that, my personal life was becoming so stressful I was struck regularly by blinding migraines that left me ill-tempered and perpetually tense like a coiled spring. I didn't have the energy to endure another semester, so the goal was simple: suck it up and get busy.

A mentor of mine from my undergrad program suggested a collection of short stories based on one I had won a Best Fiction prize for in a literary magazine during my first semester of the MFA. Desperate, I went with the idea and added poetry I had been working on prior. In eight months, I managed to conceive, write, and polish a series of stories and poetry while actively guided by one of my two writing mentors, Melissa Sanders-Self, and a fellow student whose concentration was in poetry, Jon Page.

If one of the two writing mentors assigned to me that semester (whose name I'll leave out of this foreword for reasons I'll explain later) were to read this book, she'd probably say the same insulting thing she communicated in an email after reading my first draft of the collection: Shame on you for perpetuating black stereotypes. To shame me even further, this mentor, a non-black woman, mentioned that her male black friend, a writer, would probably have a word or two with me over it. And the work in question that was the focus of the comment? A short story in my collection that was a homage to Langston Hughes' Jesse B. Semple series, a collection of columns he wrote for *The Chicago Defender*—a black-owned newspaper established in 1909 still in circulation but online—after World War II. It was the only story I wrote that wasn't geared to a specific audience like the others.

For those curious about an MFA program, listen up. In the first year and a half of my program, I read and analyzed books or documentaries that could help me form my thesis material, ones that inspired me and drove my desire to showcase my flexibility as a writer, a goal Sanders-Self inherently understood, I think. I presented these influences in the form of a bibliography that accompanied my collection along with an abstract, thesis proposal and a synopsis of works presented, formatted in Chicago Manual of Style. The entire thesis was printed on expensive archival paper, placed in an equally expensive hard-cover binder (for storage at the University's library), and submitted right before deadline to the program committee for review and acceptance. On a side note, this is the reason why an MFA is a terminal degree equal to a Ph.D.; students are held to the same standards as a Ph.D. candidate except MFAs don't have to defend a dissertation. It's the highest advanced degree that can be received in writing as a stand-alone discipline to date. And no, pursuing rhetoric and composition in a Ph.D. program is not the same! But I digress…

To say my bibliography was eclectic is an understatement. My influences included bell hooks, Stephen King, Norman Rockwell, Jhumpa Lahiri and Hughes, with other oddities thrown in. My view of Hughes was limited to his poetry and through research for books to read, I stumbled upon his Jesse B. Semple series. The writing was smooth, oh so smooth, and jazzy, introspective, sharp, funny, timeless…I gained a new appreciation for this giant of the Harlem Renaissance. Two collections of the *Chicago Defender* columns, which I still have in my personal library, were listed on my bibliography and served as an influence for my "protagonist," Franklin the hairdresser. And as I was thinking of a way to write this homage, I thought about the open conversations I had with my own hairdresser who was practically a stranger and was a character just like Jesse B. Semple; he served as a blueprint for Franklin. In truth, he's composite character of people I've encountered as I gained wisdom. And like Hughes, I use

Franklin as a conduit for highlighting some of the absurdities and contradictions in societal behavior I've always wanted to comment on.

As for the reasons why I won't disclose the name of second writing mentor, I'll name two:

1. Given our current cancel culture atmosphere, I'm sure she wouldn't want her name connected to such a cringy remark, even though she did communicate it, and

2. The email in question occurred through a now deleted email address, so my evidence is lost.

What I will say is that it was a very unlucky day for her when she chose to send that email. I couldn't allow her comments to stand unaddressed because I was offended by them; I think my immediate thought was, "How dare you!" when I finished reading it and I was eager to respond. I had just finished reading a bell hooks essay[1] for another course I was taking that semester in which bell hooks argued that as a black artist, it wasn't her responsibility to represent the black race; she challenged the term "black art." Art, she asserted, shouldn't be classified by race. When you see a Rembrandt or a Picasso, do you call it "white art"? The minute you focus on the race of the artist, the viewer's interpretation of the art shifts to racial stereotypes when analyzed or interpreted. Of course, the background of the artist is of significance because as a researcher or critic, you automatically search for clues on influences as the art is interpreted, yet historically the taint of

---

[1] bell hooks, "Art Is for Everybody," republished in the essay collection *Third Mind: Creative Writing through Visual Art* (2002) by Foster, Tonya and Kristin Prevallet.

racism at times appears to inch its way into that interpretation, especially if you threaten the status quo.

For instance, in a *New York Times* piece on a Jean-Michel Basquiat exhibition, written in May 1984 by Vivien Raynor, one of his paintings is described as such:

> In "Speaking Voice," as in a mainly blue, green and red picture of another stick figure, a female in a kerchief walking with a stick past the outline of a house, Basquiat seems to be visiting something on his subjects; it could be voodoo, for the sense of Africanness welling up is very strong…Basquiat may also have been touched by Dubuffet[2], despite being, by virtue of his Haitian background, a lot closer to the source material than the French artist is.[3]

Notice the compliment is followed by a subtle insult or peg holing based on his ethnicity, and by extension his race. Today, I guess you would call that "sneak dissing."

I think it's important to dissect the identifiers critics use to describe artists because everyone can agree that words matter and can influence a person's thinking. As an experiment, do an internet search for anything written or spoken about Picasso at the time Basquiat was active (or even currently).

---

[2] According to the MoMa website, Jean Dubuffet (1901 – 1985) was a French, "academically trained" painter, lithographer, and sculptor from a "bourgeois family" who advocated for and coined the term "art brut" ("raw art"). The website describes this term from Dubuffet as art that reflected, "instinct, passion, mood, violence, madness" and was "produced on the margins by children, outsider and folk artists, and the mentally ill."

[3] Raynor, Vivien. "Art: Paintings by Jean Michel Basquiat at Boone." *The New York Times.* May 11, 1984, Section C, Page 25.

He isn't referred to as the Iberian painter Pablo Picasso because he was born in Galicia; he's referred to as the *Spanish* painter, which is his nationality. Haitians, because of the African diaspora and the colonialism of that island, have the distinction of being an ethnonational group, a two-in-one as it were, and that group comprises descendants of Africa primarily, with a dash of the indigenous Taino population who inhabited the island prior to colonization.

To refer to Basquiat as a Haitian painter automatically conjures up black stereotypes and any perception of him as an artist worthy of examination is thrown out the window. Basquiat wasn't born in Haiti; his *nationality* is American; his *ethnicity* is half-Haitian as he is a descendant of that group on his father's side. If we wanted to hyphenate his identifier to death, Basquiat was a Haitian-Hispanic-American because his mother was from Puerto Rico.

By using such words as Haitian, voodoo and "Africanness," critics also reveal their limited knowledge of other black artists Basquiat may have been influenced by, such as Romare Bearden, Jacob Lawrence or even Hector Hyppolite, a 1940s painter from Haiti—discovered by French surrealist André Breton—who was suspected of being a descendant of a vodou (voodoo) priest[4]. These artists have recurring motifs similar to what Raynor describes in "Speaking Voice." Comparisons to Bearden or Hyppolite for the use of bold colors would have been more appropriate if Basquiat's art was to be critiqued under the umbrella of Africa. Equally disconcerting is the mention of Jean Dubuffet, and Basquiat being "closer to the source material"

---

[4] "Hector Hyppolite." MoMA.org

because he's Haitian (see footnote 2). One might view this as an attempt to legitimize Basquiat by comparing his work to more established, accepted white artists while at the same time hinting at its folkish, seemingly amateur composition. Granted, Basquiat was originally a graffiti artist and was expressing what saw through the lens of a black man in America. And artists are often compared to others when describing how an artist uses shape, color, technique, etc. But in reviews of Basquiat's work at the time he was active, all written or spoken by white critics, his blackness or being Haitian appeared to be the one thing some critics relied on to describe, critique, and interpret.

Though Basquiat was unable address his critics directly, I sure as hell was! In a long, *heated* email back to that mentor, written at 1 am by the glow of my laptop, I used bell hooks' argument to basically say, "Shame on you for making me responsible for my race." We had limited contact from there on out. Knowledge really is power, people!

But I did have a good mentor in Sanders-Self. She gave excellent edits to tease more out of me and because I trusted her, I incorporated them. However, for the short story "A Perfect Day for A Haircut," which introduced the Franklin character, her edits were rejected, but not by me. The rejection came from a group of people that neither she, nor I expected feedback from.

In my last semester of grad school, I was on a tight schedule with writing and revising my short stories and poetry. One could say I was on an Agile schedule. I gave myself three-week sprints for every "iteration," alternating between the prose and poetry. This was a work process I picked up from my time as a ghost writer for romance magazines in the late '90s. The minute I was done with a story, I would email it to Sanders-Self and then immediately start on the idea for the next story (the same process was done for the poetry portion with Jon Page, my fellow grad student). She would print it out, do a pen-and-ink markup and then we would talk about her edits over the phone (she lived and taught in California at the time; I was on the East coast).

According to Sanders-Self, she had printed out the Haircut story to edit while she was under the dryer at her hairdressers. In haste, she left the marked-up pages behind with minor edits. When she realized she had lost the pages, she retraced her steps to the hairdressers and picked them up about a week later. The employee who handed it back to her told her everyone had read the story and nobody agreed with her edits. The story should stay exactly as it was written was the consensus; I had captured a day in the life of a hairdressers accurately.

Sometimes, life truly is stranger than fiction.

It was the ultimate validation for me, as a writer, to have a group of complete strangers read *a first draft* and say don't change a thing. That's the stuff you see in movies, not in real life. To this day, I wonder if Sanders-Self left those pages behind on purpose to test audience reaction. Nevertheless, I realized that I had struck a chord with my accuracy. No, not accuracy…it was the *sincerity*.

That's why Hughes' work resonated with me; it wasn't disingenuous, and it had mass appeal. After all, the columns were published via the most well-used medium at the time next to radio: newspapers, so they were written to maintain readership while subversively speaking to values that people could relate to, that I related to. He clearly understood David Berlo's SMCR Model of Communication[5] by coding his message of values and observations through a fictional character, Jesse B. Semple, a regular-smegular guy from around the way whom everyone called "Simple" as one of those sneak disses I talked about earlier. In Hughes' foreword for *The Best of Simple,* he stated he wrote the character to be someone everyone knew and many who approached him would claim they knew a person who was a real-life Jesse B. Semple. This shows how much the column rang true for many readers, hence its popularity at the time. And somehow, 60+ years later, a little black girl from Queens, New York, who read incessantly to escape her lonely childhood during the weirdness of the '70s and '80s, managed to successfully generate that same frankness and it resonated with a small group of hairdressers in a shop 3,000 miles away.

Here we are, over a decade since I graduated and I'm writing this foreword for a book on a character I've created, one who I'd like to think would be besties with Jesse B. Semple.

I know some people might think, "Isn't this a rip off from that Ice Cube movie Barbershop? Or that Queen Latifah movie Beauty Shop?" The setting is similar, yes. But honestly, I was searching for an occupation where these types of conversations would occur, and I thought a beauty parlor is one of those rare places where people are open about their lives; you can't hide your troubles from a hairdresser! It's a

---

[5] Berlo's SMCR Model of Communication, a framework for the transmission of information, includes four components: sender, message, channel, and receiver. The values of the sender and receiver should be alike for successful communication.

great setting to emulate those one-on-one, in-depth conversations better versus a group free for all. I wanted the focus on the discourse between Franklin and the unnamed narrator and create a time capsule. Plus, it tickles me to write a character against stereotypes of male hairdressers. Assumptions run rampant when men serve in traditional "pink" occupations.

Hopefully this book is worthy of a break from social media or streaming services. I can't definitively say I know who the audience for this book is and I didn't write it as I was singing the old Coca-Cola commercial about how I'd like to buy the world a Coke. The audience, my friends, is anyone with a mind, heart and soul who's willing to listen for a while. The past isn't as bad as we pretend it to be; keep an open mind. And please feel free to laugh. No one is around to judge you.

Roles of Men and Women

Franklin will tell his story to anyone who is willing to listen. Actually, the word "willing" is fluid, for those who sit in his chair have no choice but to do so. To pass the time as hair get curled, cut or processed until it's bone-straight, the female has to listen and respond to make the conversation meaningful and, to be honest, less boring.

Franklin has seen it all and done it all, and he laments over the passing of those good times as though he has one foot in the grave. He has clearly reached the wrong side of 60, but if you attempt to extract a specific number from him, your attempts will be thwarted. He stands at six feet plus, with a butter pecan tan complexion and brown eyes hidden behind thick lenses. Sporting a smooth-shaven head and a salt-and-pepper goatee, he's a lanky individual, size 36 waist most probably and his spindly arms are adorned with tattoos. He was at the peak of his manhood during the 1970's and he reflects on that time wistfully, though some of the women in his chair may find his nostalgia offensive as it pertains to the roles of women.

"I don't know what's up with you women today," Franklin says as he takes a little hair off the top of my head. Being it is my first time in his chair (my previous hairdresser retired), I take this comment with a grain of salt and a grain of hope that the conversation will not turn into one that will evoke my swift tongue.

"You women are always busy. You always got somewhere to go. You at work, or you got to run somewhere for somethin', or you got church duties. You don't have time for your man and you can't slow down."

"Don't forget school and kids," I offer as he gently pushes my head down to cut hairs along the neckline.

"Yeah, yeah," he agrees. He stops for a moment to check his progress before he continues. "School, kids, work, church…seems like you women are trying to purposely keep your lives full. Ain't havin' a man enough for you?"

I can feel my tongue ready to strike, but I am ever cognizant of the fact that the success of my hairdo rests on his angular shoulders. Back-up hairdressers are difficult to find.

"A woman has to have something for herself," I reason. "I hear horror stories all the time of women who give all to their man, the man leaves and she has nothing."

"Hmmm," he mutters as he tips my head to the side once more.

"I know one woman who married a man she knew was wrong for her after the first year of marriage. *The first year!* She still stayed with him. Had three children by him one right after the other…boom, boom, boom. No time for rest."

"So what happened?"

"She quit college, mistake number one. She stayed married to him for 15 years and sort of ignored what he was truly all about, mistake number two. Then one summer he filed for divorce and left her. They were having problems before then, but she never thought he would up and leave her with the kids. She had it in her mind that he would act like an honorable man, especially since they were married for so long. So now she's struggling as a single parent, got bills up the ying yang…doesn't have anything for herself, not even time to find a little peace."

Franklin comes around to the front to do a spot check of his handiwork. He hands me a mirror and asks if my neckline is cut the way I like it. He turns my chair so the mirror in my hand offers a reflection of my neckline off the wall mirror.

"Oh yeah," I say, smoothing the hairs. "That's nice. A scarf can make that lie flat."

"You sure you don't want the clippers?"

"Naw, man. You got it right." He nods and takes the mirror from my hand.

"So that's why you think women keep busy, huh?" he asks, picking up our line of conversation.

"I'm no expert, but I think women need to have something for themselves."

"Like I said before, ain't havin' a man enough?"

"Do you think the fact that a man is hanging around is enough to keep a woman satisfied with her life? Should you men get a special award for it?"

"Naw, that ain't what I'm sayin'…" he begins.

"That it's a sin for a woman to get hers if she wants it?"

"Hold on," he laughs. "You misunderstandin' me…"

"I don't get you men," I continue as he dips my head to the side again to perfect his cut. "We women are damned if we do and damned if we don't. If we sit around and wait on you hand and foot, we're smothering you and all of a sudden you're screaming you need space—"

"No woman has ever waited on me hand and foot! I can say that for sure! Name one black woman you know who waits on her man."

"I can name several."

"Then give me their phone number so I can hollah at 'em."

He directs me out of the chair and over to the row of ebony sinks to wash my hair. As sharp streams of warm water hit my dirty hair, Franklin's magic fingers vigorously scrub my greasy scalp and I can feel my neck muscles relax under his ministrations.

"This is how I see it," he shouts above the din of the water spray. "I've been married four times and God willin', this fourth marriage will be my last. But—"

"Hold on a sec," I shout back. "You've been married four times and you haven't figured out black women yet?"

Franklin laughs. "I ain't sayin' it's all their fault on the marriage-fallin'-apart thing. I have my faults too—"

"I'm glad you can admit to that, but go on with what you were saying."

"What was I sayin'?" he says as he rinses my hair and applies conditioner. "Oh…I've been married four times. All good women. All of them helped me clean myself up. My second wife got me into rehab when I was strung out on that heroin, took me out of that environment so I could make a new start. That's how I wound up in Hartford."

Franklin rinses out the conditioner, wraps my head in a towel and guides me back to his styling station.

"My third wife," he continues, "Sent me to beautician's school, paid for it out of her pocket and helped me get set up for my shop. And she was a single mom, too."

"What about your first wife?" I ask.

"Good woman, also. She got me to settle down from my wild ways. Sort of set up the scene for my second wife to continue the missionary work, if you catch what I'm sayin'."

"Franklin," I say as he runs a comb through my wet hair. "You're kind of proving my point here."

"Hold on, I ain't finished."

He stops and eyes my damp hair before he grabs his scissors to cut loose ends.

"My first three wives, they really took care of me and I wanted to take care of them."

"And did you?"

"Naw, they never gave me the chance. They were too busy bein' my mother instead of my wife. And I was bad, I let them do it. But then the marriage reached a point where I was ready for them to be my wife and they didn't know how to."

"And whose fault is that?"

"Nobody's, I guess. That's just how it happened."

"No discussion?"

"Yeah, there was discussion, but it was too late. How does it sound for a man to say, 'Honey, stop doin' stuff for me.' Try tellin' that to a black woman and she starts supposin' stuff."

"Supposing what stuff?"

"Like," he says as he puts his scissors away. "Why? 'Why all of sudden you tellin' me to stop?' 'Is there another woman givin' you somethin' I ain't givin' you'…that kind of stuff."

"Now you're talkin' crazy talk," I joke as he adds a wrapping lotion to my hair.

"Come on now. You know what I'm sayin' is true."

"Franklin, you are contradicting yourself…left and right, man. You said before that no woman has waited on you—"

"That's true."

"But you said—"

"My ex-wives never waited on me. They mothered me. That ain't the same as waiting on me. They were fixin' me."

"Didn't you need to be fixed?"

"No lie, yeah I did. But if the entire marriage is about fixin' me, then problems start. I didn't need another mother, the one I had was just fine, God rest her soul."

"So back to the wives situation," I say as he is smoothing my hair around my head with a fine-toothed comb. "The first three tried to fix you. What about your current wife?"

"Oh, I love her to death," he says with a broad smile. "She's a little younger than me, but age ain't nothin' but a number."

"Uh huh," is my reply.

"Anyway," he says, lightly smacking the side of my head in a playful nature. "She ain't interested in fixin' me. She let me know from jump street she didn't have time to fix me so if I was broke, take it somewhere else."

"And you liked that," I say, more as a statement.

"Yeah I liked that. She laid out the rules and I was down to follow 'em."

"But…?"

"But," he says as he molds wrapping paper around my head to adhere to the wrapping lotion. "I ain't use to those kind of rules, man! She's a paralegal at a big law firm so she works late…a lot. So now I have to take on this role…you know…keepin' the house in order, caring for our daughter…stuff like that."

"You mean women's work."

"Now why you tryin' to put words in my mouth, woman!" he says as he secures the wrapping paper with a clip. "All's I'm sayin' is I had to take on a role I didn't play with my ex-wives and it took time for me to adjust."

"Why don't you just come on out with it. Call a spade a spade. You have a problem with your wife taking on a more…what are the words I'm looking for? A more aggressive role in the relationship."

"Aggressive role? What's that mean?"

"I'm using the wrong word. I mean…a more dominant role. She's out working late in corporate America and you're at home taking care of things."

"I don't have a problem with doin' what I have to do to keep things in order. Go with the flow, don't fight it, that's where the trouble starts. Tryin' to control a situation, tryin' to control people and how they think, it's useless. Besides all that, I went into the marriage with eyes wide open. It's too late for me to flip now."

"Um…," I utter thoughtfully.

"Are you a spiritual person? You go to church?"

"No, I don't do anything like that."

"Why not?"

"Well, I don't believe in paying someone for my redemption and salvation," I say.

"I don't get you."

"Ok, for example," I began. "One early Saturday morning some missionaries from a local church, two young kids, rang my doorbell to ask me if I go to church or read scripture. When I told them what I told you, they asked me what I was going to tell God on my judgment day."

"And what did you say?"

"I said I would tell God that although I didn't know the Bible word-for-word and didn't visit his house of worship, I tried to live my life by the spirit of the teachings within, that I tried to live a decent life, be good to other people and treat them as I would like to be treated. What I didn't add is that sometimes, it's hard for me to do that on a consistent basis when people pluck my last nerve with their nonsense. My husband is a walking, talking nerve plucker, let me tell you!"

"And what did they say to that?"

"'Good answer!' And do you know they still tried to get me to their church? I told them it's too late, brother, you already proved I am good to go on my own."

"Did you mean what you said?" he asks.

"I meant every word. Why go to church, tithe, listen to a sermon from someone else's interpretation of what I need to do to obtain salvation, praise God and then sin for the rest of the week until the next Sunday cleanses me? I'm not against churches, I'm not against religion. Everybody needs a little faith."

"What about those that don't sin?"

"God bless 'em, because they are better than I am. If they can listen to the word and do well not only in one week but throughout their lifetime, then they have a sure place beside God's throne. I'll have to do some negotiation when I hit the pearly gates and that's assuming my soul will have the option of using the 'up' escalator."

Franklin eases me out of his chair to the bonnet hair dryer where he cranks up the heat to a respectable level and I enjoy the quiet the dryer provides, dozing off from time-to-time. He checks on me periodically until, after 30 minutes, he deems my hair dry enough to proceed to the styling portion of my visit.

"Do *you* go to church?" I ask, picking up the thread of conversation where it left off.

"When I can," he says. "I'm a very spiritual person. Are you?"

"I believe in a higher power, yes. I believe that there is someone…up there, somewhere, guiding our actions, looking out for us. We need help sometimes, don't we?"

"Man, ain't that the truth. I know a lot of people that need help."

On the counter behind Franklin sits a complicated contraption that stores his large collection of old-fashioned curling irons and straightening combs. I am familiar with these irons; many a Sunday my grandmother would heat a straightening comb on her gas stove to give my nappy head the cute bangs and pigtails that made me feel so special before she dragged me to church for a painfully long sermon I never understood. The oven that heats these curling irons to the level of giving a third-degree burn and singeing hair to a smelly stubble, is positioned at the base of this contraption. He takes a small-sized curling iron out of the oven and proceeds to curl my short hair one small section at a time.

"So, what you got goin' on in your life?" Franklin asks me.

"A more accurate question is what I *don't* have going on. I'm one of those busy women you were complaining about earlier."

"And why do you keep yourself so busy?"

I pause to contemplate his question, and then respond, "I guess to prove I was here, on this earth."

"Ain't the fact that you were born enough?"

"Should I sit on the sidelines and watch other people?"

"Don't mean you have to kill yourself to prove you were here. Life ain't about all that."

"I'm not killing myself. I'm sitting in your chair, right? I'm not struck with illness. Yes, I'm stressed, but no more than other people."

"Yeah, but is all this activity worth it? What does your *husband* feel about all this busy-ness?"

"He knew what I had going on in the fire when he met and married me. If he had expectations that marriage was going to slow me down, then that's on him. To be fair, he does help out around the house, he cooks better than I do, does a little cleaning when the spirit moves him. He keeps a job, that's the main thing."

"Oh, here we go," Franklin says, using the curling iron with quick efficiency. "Black-men-keepin'-a-job nonsense. Angry black woman on the floor!"

"No, it's not nonsense. Rent, electric, gas, water…there is no place on this earth where all that stuff is free. The U.S.A. isn't a socialist country; it's a *capitalist* country and a dog-eat-dog society. If you were living on your own and you didn't bother to pay the basics, you'd come home to a freezing place, dark as hell, can't flush the toilet and an eviction notice on your door, simple as that. It's not unreasonable to expect my spouse or any man living with me to pay his share, and in order to do that you need to keep a damn job."

"Hey, I know women who don't do their share, always on the look out for some sugar daddy to rescue 'em. Pay their bills, give 'em a little money to get their hair and nails done…"

"Don't bite the hand that feeds you," I say.

"You don't hear men yellin' that women need to keep a job."

"That's because men expect women to stay home so they can be the breadwinner."

"Naw, sistah. You got it wrong. Men *want* women to work 'cause we don't need all the stress of being responsible for everythin'. If you women want to take a front seat, we'll sure as hell let you."

"But see one roach in the kitchen and the man starts bitchin' about the woman not keeping the place clean. My husband had the nerve to do that one day when *one* roach showed up in our kitchen…he just stood there and pointed at it like a pointer Collie flushing out game, plus he had that look on his face."

"What look?" Franklin asks, stopping to look me in the eye.

"That accusatory look…like it was my fault the roach was there, like if I had cleaned that small glob of ice cream I left on the counter one night or sponged off the crumbs from my morning toast, the roach wouldn't be there."

"You women are so sensitive…always lookin' into something that ain't there," he says as he resumes his styling. "My wife does that, tryin' to read my mind, like our marriage certificate gave her some special power. Did he come out and say it was your fault?"

"He didn't have to, I know that look. Now mind you, that was the first and only roach in our house—"

"You mean so far."

"I mean *only*! But somehow that one roach sighting cast a bad glow on my housekeeping abilities."

"Well, how'd the roach get there?" he asks.

"I have *no* idea. Our house was pest-free when we moved in. Personally, I think he brought the roach into the house and trained it to come out on cue so he could hold something over me."

"It's all in your mind. You probably lettin' your guilt get the best of you."

"My guilt over what?" I say, spinning around in my chair to face him.

"For lettin' all this *busy-ness* get in the way of doin' what you should be doin'"

"Which is?"

"Takin' care of your man," he says with a grin.

"I don't recall my wedding vows saying anything about 'taking care of my man,'" I say, settling back in my chair. "Did yours?"

"If you knew my wife, you'd know she don't play that kind of nonsense. She's quick to tell me there's only *one* child in the house, and that's our daughter."

"That's what I thought. Anyway, my point is a partnership shouldn't be lopsided, both should contribute *equally*."

"What does the roach situation have to do with partnership?"

"That you say men want us to take the driver's seat, but you give us the evil fish eye when we can't keep all the balls in the air. Step up to the plate every once in a while…clean up that glob of ice cream, wipe off a toast crumb or two, it's not going to make you any less of a man, whatever being a man means," I say.

"Listen, I ain't hung up on all that 'being a man' nonsense. Shoot…I help out in my house—"

"Because you'd never hear the end of it if you didn't."

"No, I do it because like you said, a partnership should be equal."

"Then leave some DNA behind so you can be cloned, okay?"

"What I have a problem with," he says as he tips my head sideways to carefully curl an area close to my ear. "Are those women lookin' for a sugar daddy, want everything done for 'em. They come up in here and talk about how their man bought them this and that, talkin' about how they gonna kick their man to the curb if they don't pay their cell phone bill or get them that wavy hair extension…"

"Like I said before, there is nothing on this earth that's free. Everything comes with a price, even being at some man's beck and call for a little cash."

"So if a rich man came up to you and offered to buy you a house, a car, pay your bills, the whole nine if you'd slip him some sweetness when he needs it, you'd turn him down?" he asks, meeting my eye.

I snort audibly at his question and say, "My theory on that is this: a man will only stay with a cow if the milk is tasty. The minute he thinks the milk tastes sour, he'll split and find another cow with better milk. Notice I say 'tastes sour' not 'getting sour.' That milk may be at the peak of goodness with every milking. But if it tastes like piss to *him*, it's time for him to go."

"You speakin' from experience or somethin'?"

"Don't be in my business!" I quip back. "But I will say I've never had a sugar daddy. All the men in my life, with the exclusion of my husband, never paid my bills even when they were getting all the sweetness they could handle."

"Oh, so your husband pays the bills, huh?"

"We split the responsibility. I never want to be beholden to any man. But let's get real here. He has no choice in the matter. He couldn't watch ESPN if he didn't."

"He can get his news off the Internet," Franklin interjects.

"Not if the cable and electric bills aren't paid, he can't."

"I couldn't be married to you, you're too tough. All this feminist talk is givin' me the hives."

"No, all the truth I'm laying down for you is giving you the hives. You better hope I don't run into your wife one day," I say, wagging a finger at him.

"I'm gonna make it my business that you two don't meet."

"Don't fight the truth, brothah man. Just surrender."

Franklin is done with the curling session. He gently combs out the curls into the style I told him I would like, and then walks around my head to tweak a piece of hair this way and that to get the sassy look he thinks will please. He hums a song I don't recognize as he does this. When he's done, he hands me a mirror to look at the back, front and sides. I am pleased. I settle the bill and give him a decent tip, and then schedule my next appointment in three weeks.

"I usually kiss my clients before they go," Franklin says with a cheeky smile as I prepare myself to leave.

"Not today you're not."

"Don't worry, I wasn't goin' to do that to you. You bein' a feminist and everythin'"

"Correction: I'm an antireligious feminist who believes in tipping, remember that," I say, returning his smile.

The Loss of Manners

It has been a while since I've seen Franklin. When I call to schedule an appointment, he gives me the address of his new location in a different town. His new location shares the space with a bustling barbershop, and I find the space to be a nice change from where I saw him last. The location, which is on a busy street in a mixed-zone section of town, is split in half and both sides have mounted flat screen TVs playing at low levels; sports on one side, talk and game shows on the other. As usual, Franklin is the only male hairdresser, something he has no complaints about. If ever there was a human version of a rooster enjoying the hen house, it was Franklin. He chats and flirts with the other beauticians he works alongside and due to his gregarious nature and attractiveness, they subtly flirt back.

A new location apparently brings new clientele, which leads to appointments overlapping. Being new to the world of having a regular hairdresser, I find waiting 15 minutes when I've arrived on time a bit annoying, like arriving on time for a doctor's appointment and waiting even though you were threatened with a cancellation fee for lateness. He finally calls me over to his chair after he's placed a client under a hairdryer.

"How you doin' today?" says Franklin with a smile as he places a cape around my neck. He then runs his fingers through my dirty hair to assess my situation.

"Pretty good. I like the new location."

"Yeah, this works better for me. I'm closer to home, makes it easier for my wife to pick me up."

"You don't drive?"

"Oh, I drive. But I don't have a license."

"You don't have a license? There's a story in there somewhere. How do you get to work?"

"On my bike."

"You mean a motorcycle?"

"No, I mean a 10-speed bike. I ride my bike home, but on bad weather days, my wife will get me."

"You're kidding me."

"Naw, I'm serious. I ride my bike when I can, other times my wife will drive me."

"Don't you worry about someone stealing it?"

"Nope." He points to a corner of the room where I spot for the first time a bicycle front wheel. I nod my head to show my admiration. This bit of knowledge about Franklin explains his slim, athletic frame.

He takes a wide-toothed comb from his workstation and begins parting my hair this way and that before he pronounces it's time for a touch-up relaxer, which I agree to. He then begins to prep my scalp for the chemical paste he will soon apply. As he walks around me to apply Vaseline to the edges of my hair, I accidently raise my elbow, making contact with his side. I immediately apologize.

"You're good," he responds, "no need to say sorry."

"I disagree. Intentional or unintentional, I should apologize."

"And why is that?"

"Because people have forgotten manners, that's why. Civility is gone! I feel like I need to be civil and polite everywhere I go, to remind people that once upon a time, we used to say things like sorry, excuse me, thank you—"

"I hear you, I hear you," he says as he parts my hair in quarters. "My little girl is beginning to pick up bad habits from all these other kids. I see it in the way she sometimes talks to my wife. I had to remind her how things work in my house."

"Did you go full-on old school or did you stop short of the belt?"

Franklin snorts a laugh. "Had to stop short of the belt. The wife don't like me laying hands on a child. That ain't her thing. There's no 'spare the rod and spoil the child' in her house. She's all about doin' the opposite of how her parents raised her."

"I can understand that. It's a form of discipline no kid has fond memories of. At school, I was sent to the corner to face the wall. Humiliating! At home it was the belt. Painful! No kid deliberately did something wrong so they could get a beat down with a belt. If they did, they were at the beginnings of being a masochist or probably already flipped into one."

"Which was worse, you think? The belt or the iron cord? I ran from both."

"Yeah, they both run neck-and-neck in the pain department", I agree. "But that cord?…woo! And then there might be hanging line involved, like that line for hanging clothes, the one you used to play hot peas and butter with—"

"You takin' me back now. I remember when a neighbor caught me sayin' certain words I had no business sayin'," reminisces Franklin.

"What words?"

"What you think?" he asks. "Cuss words! I was cussin' up a storm over somethin' or other, showin' off for my friends. Neighbor heard me and went to my grandma and told her everything. Got home that night and it was *not* a good night, lemme tell you! I had welts for a couple of days. After that, I kept my cussin' to a minimum, at least around grown folk!"

"There you go! Cussin' isn't civil; it's rude, so you had people around you to check you," I say.

"Oh yeah. Back then people looked out for other people's kids, you know? If a neighbor said something to you, it was the same as if your family was talkin' to you. So, you watched yourself 'cause you never knew who was watchin'. But here's the thing: Where you think I learned those cuss words?"

"I know where I learned mine!" I joke.

"From your family, right?"

"Yes, sir!" I say with a laugh.

"Exactly. Family gets together, someone gets liquored up, and before you know it Uncle So-and-So is cussin' here, there, and everywhere in front of us kids. Everybody's feelin' too good to correct him or tell him to clean up his language 'cause kids can hear; they're too busy laughin' and havin' a good time. And what do us kids do? We repeat what we hear!

We wanna feel grown and if the grown-ups are sayin' those words, and they ain't correctin' us, then us kids can say 'em, right?"

"That's the logic," I agree.

"Don't get me wrong, I don't like little kids sayin' cuss words. I can look at it from the adult side and see how that don't look good. That's *too* grown. You know that phrase we use when we see a kid actin' up."

"No home training," is my reply.

"What we need right now is good home *and* neighborhood trainin'! But it starts at home and you gotta lay down the law in your house and live by it, and that's what I do with my daughter. If you tellin' your kids don't cuss, then you can't cuss around 'em!"

"Set the example," I say.

"Right! Set the example of how you want your kids to behave. I will say this…you can do your best with your kids at home, but the minute they step out that door into the neighborhood, everything you try to do can be undone quick! That's why I say we need neighborhood trainin' too."

"I kinda agree with your wife, though," I say, "not doing corporal punishment. We didn't like it when we were kids, so why do that to ours? Besides, nowadays, that's considered child abuse and *nobody* wants child services at their door telling them they're abusive parents."

"Well, my track record in the parenting department ain't the greatest, so I do what the wife wants, child services or no."

"Why is that?" I ask.

"'Cause I wasn't around much for my kids. I got six of 'em."

"Wait, hold up, you have six kids?"

"Yup."

"You mean between your three ex-wives and your current wife you have six kids?" I ask, turning my head to meet his gaze.

"Well, not exactly," he responds with a grin.

"What *exactly* is not exactly?"

"I should back up a sec. With my current daughter, I have seven kids total."

"I'm with you so far."

"Two of those kids are from my first marriage. One is from my second marriage. My youngest of the seven, my daughter, is from my current marriage. The rest—"

"Ahhhh, no further explanation required," I say, turning my head back. "Are you close with all of them?"

"Not all of them. I've been workin' on that. My oldest just turned 40. One did a little jail time, but overall they're all doin' well despite the fact that I wasn't around for them as much as I should've been. My mom wasn't happy about that."

"Having come from a single parent home and being a single parent at one time, I can see why."

"Yeah, my mom was quick to remind me how my papa was a rollin' stone when I wasn't doin' what I was supposed to be doin' for them. That why with my little girl, things are different. I'm there, ya know, doin' the parentin', puttin' in the work. But …you know…I'm on a learning curve with that."

"At the very least, you cover manners."

"Oh, yeah I do, but a belt ain't a part of how I handle it. It's a good thing I don't do what my mom would do if my little girl ever sassed my mom the way she's sassed my wife sometimes. You can bet that girl would be feeling a belt, an iron cord, a hand…sometimes all three!"

I can feel the cool paste being applied on my hair at the scalp. He works quickly and efficiently to work the four quarters of my head, using an applicator brush. Breaking the silence, I say,

"Just the other day I was at Staples to mail a package and it was busy, so I waited my turn, you know, just standing there quietly. She acknowledged that I'm there, she saw me, so I just figured I'd wait because I didn't have to be anywhere important. When she finally gets to me, she thanked me for being so patient and I shrugged my shoulders like it was no big deal. I said to her, 'I'm just being polite' and do you know what she said?"

"What?"

"She said, 'Don't you know that being impolite is the new polite?'"

"She's right about that," Franklin agrees before lowering his voice. "Sometimes these women will cuss me out if something ain't done the way they like it. Or they run their mouth about how much I'm chargin' when they've been comin' to me for years. But they don't think twice about not showin' up on time or not even showin' up; no phone call, no warnin'. I don't do this for free. This is how I make my money. There's only so many customers I can fit in one day and that's why there's overlap. People think they can say or do whatever they want to you—"

"And forget you have feelings," I interrupt.

"They do! And they don't say sorry or nothin'. They'll come back as though they never cussed me out or did somethin' wrong the last time I saw them. And you know you want to say somethin'—"

"But because they're a client," I say, "you keep your mouth shut."

"I do. I've learned to let that stuff roll off my back. You don't know what they was goin' through at that time, ya know? They might have somethin' serious goin' on and forgot they had an appointment. Or they couldn't leave what was botherin' them at home, so they took it out on me that day, who knows? But for me, if I was havin' a bad day and took it out on someone, I would say sorry the minute I saw them again. I'm an Aquarius; I like to get along with everybody. Can't let that negative energy linger with people."

"But even if a person is having a bad day and has something going on in their life, does that mean they have the right to ruin other people's day? I have absolutely no patience with those type of people."

"You just as bad as they are!" he says as he tilts my head forward to smooth down the hair at the nape of my neck.

"I guess. Maybe. No, there's a difference," I say. "My impatience comes from their rudeness, not because I'm being held up from leaving or my life has turned to crap. That person made a decision at that moment to shit all over someone else's day. You can argue that person might be in physical pain or emotional pain…whatever. Still doesn't make it right. And nine times out of ten, it's *your* generation that's being rude. That's a headscratcher to me."

"My generation! What you got against my generation?" he asks, tapping my head playfully.

"Ya'll just seem to be bitter over everything! Determined to suck out the joy everywhere you go. I wanna know what you all are so bitter about? I know most of you were raised by the silent generation and I know you got smacked in the face with manners; it was part of your upbringing."

"It was," concedes Franklin. "You *knew* there was a church voice, an outdoor voice, an indoor voice, a school voice, etc. If you messed up and forgot which voice to use depending on where you were or who you were with—"

"You got smacked, right?" I say.

"Not gonna lie, when I was growin' up, how you acted in the streets was a reflection on how you was raised. Mrs. So-and-So gave you some little change to get some penny candy at the corner store, you better say thank you to Mrs. So-and-So! When you say thank you, that's you showin' gratitude, showin' people you were raised right. We never questioned it," says Franklin.

"Is that why your generation is such a dark cloud everywhere you go? Because ya'll were forced to do things and caught hell if you didn't?"

"Why you broad strokin'?"

"I'm just trying to understand why a generation of people who were raised on being polite walk around so grumpy! I mean…we all got dragged to church back then…"

"Yes, we did," agrees Franklin.

"There was never a question of *not* saying please or thank you, or *not* keeping your indoor voice indoors. Never. And your generation raised mine so the expectation for politeness was passed on. When you have manners, or demonstrate manners, you're showing you consider other people. But I think it goes beyond just saying please and thank you. People don't have patience anymore; they want things to happen immediately and when they don't—"

"They get nasty," interrupts Franklin. "I saw a road rage incident that had me shook!"

"Road rage, black Friday after Thanksgiving, fast food window transactions that go sideways, you name it. You go on social media and there's videos of people losing their 'effin' minds. Granted, I do see my generation acting stupid at times, or the younger generation. But every time I go into a store and there's an issue, it's your generation holding up the line."

"That's 'cause we don't like foolishness from someone who don't know their job, that's why!" he says. "You can't even pay stuff with cash 'cause they don't know how to make change. They look like they strugglin', tryin' to figure out subtraction. You notice there's change makin' machines at fast food places? That's 'cause companies would lose money with those kids behind the counter."

"But why be disagreeable?" I ask. "It's a mystery to me because manners were something expected while your generation was growing up."

"Everybody has their breakin' point! Some reach that point sooner than others."

"I won't disagree with you on that," I reply. "But I'll tell you something. I'm not gonna lie and say I don't enjoy those videos of people who get instant payback for acting stupid, instant karma these kids call it. I'm like, good, that's what you get for being a rude idiot. Your car flipped over for trying to cut off a person in the pouring rain? Sucks to be you."

Franklin chuckles as he smooths the chemical paste about my head with the spine of a rattail comb and tells me to let him know when my scalp starts tingling. It doesn't take long before I start to feel the tingle and signal to him that it's time to rinse the paste out. He brings me to a sink and I lay back to gratefully receive the strong spray of slightly hot water that he runs over my head as though I am being baptized.

This is the quiet portion of the visit for us. With strong, slender fingers he massages the neutralizing shampoo into my hair, which relaxes me and I stop fighting his fingers on my scalp; my head begins to loll from side to side as he continues his vigorous scrubbing. Another rinse of water and then he applies the conditioner to gently rub into my hair, to be followed by a last rinse of water. He pats my hair dry and then leads me back to his chair. Franklin combs out my wet hair, walks around the chair to survey my hair before going back to his work counter to grab a pair of scissors. He tilts my head and begins to cut.

"There was one time when this old dude took it too far with the rudeness," I say suddenly as he works around my head.

"Why? What happened?"

"I was on a company shuttle bus, which was basically an old school bus painted over. We got to the building and even though the bus stopped, no one was getting up to leave; meanwhile, I'm in the back of the bus, and yes, I'm the only black person back there. I'm already late for where I had to be, I had to go to the bathroom really bad, and nobody's moving! So, I'm like, forget this! I got up to move towards the front. This white dude, *about your age*, elbows me to keep me from leaving before everyone else, whining that bus protocol is like deboarding a plane."

Franklin stops to face me and looks over the top of his glasses. "What you mean he elbows you?"

"He raises his elbow," I say, demonstrating the action, "and presses it into my hip, really hard, to keep me from moving."

"And what did you do?"

"I pushed past him, his elbow and his cheap coat and said we're not on a plane. I'm from New York where we don't give a shit about protocol. If we need to get off a bus or a train, we do it."

"What happened then?"

"I got off the damn bus! I was not in the mood that day. What I should've done was threaten to sit on his lap."

"Sit on his lap! That ain't a threat from where I stand."

"Well, at that time I was on my period and I'm a heavy bleeder."

Franklin shakes his head before he says somberly, "You know that had nothin' to do with…bus protocol or a…a…generation thing, right?"

"Oh, I know."

Franklin goes back to work to finish the cut and then applies wrapping lotion to my hair, smoothing it out with a comb about my head.

"Huh! You better than I am," says Tasha, the beautician in the booth next to us who overhears our conversation. "Some old white man put any part of his body on mine he's not supposed to and I'm knockin' him the hell out!"

"How would I look if I did that, though?" I say. "A young black female wildin' out on an old white man on a company bus? How do you think that story will play out on social media?"

"How it's gonna play?" Tasha says. "You gonna look like the hood rat people think we all are, that's how. You can't win."

"If you defend yourself, you in the wrong," Franklin chimes in. "It don't matter what happened before it. That's how most will see it."

"A female waaaay grimier than me might've broken out the knife that she keeps in her purse for times like those and cut him."

"I know that's right!" Tasha replies a beat later, a grin on her face.

The Old Days

In the New England states, the weather can become unpredictable after a certain point in the new year. Halfway through the month of April, the temperature high is 60° when it would normally be in the upper 40s as the area transitions to spring. I find this temperature spike to be annoying in more ways than one because dressing becomes difficult; last week I was wearing layers and now I am forced to dress light.

"You got the fans on in here," I say to Franklin as I settle down in his chair.

"Yeah, man. With all these hairdryers and summer weather goin' on, you can't sit in here without sweatin'."

"Ain't it crazy? I'm going to get sick; I just know it," I say.

"I almost put on a tank top, but I thought better of it."

"Explain to me why I'm seeing booty shorts for a few days of warm weather?"

Franklin laughs before saying, "I got nothin' to say on that issue!"

"It's an honest question. I'm seeing booty shorts, spaghetti tank tops with the *so-called* shelf bra, boobs swaying here and there, and those godforsaken slides and flip flops, two of the most damaging footwear for foot arches. That flap! flap! flap! drives me nuts."

"How old did you say you were?" Franklin asks

"I didn't say."

"Are you over 65?" jokes Franklin.

"Look, I don't have to be over 65 to complain about booty shorts. I look at old pictures of Harlem, like from the 30s and 40s, and people dressed to impress back then. The men, always in a suit or a shirt, tie, and pants combo; hair laid down, clean shaven, shoes shined. Even the non-formal stuff for men was fly, those V-neck sweaters or short-sleeved button downs. Women didn't step out of their door without their dresses clean and pressed, hair looking fly, hats just right, cute kid gloves. And they weren't rich people.

Back then, pantyhose and half-slips weren't ancient pieces of clothing. Do you know the only stores that sell garters are sexy lingerie shops? Good luck finding half-slips. When I was growing up, I could go to Macy's or A&S or any department store and find all kinds of undergarments, from full slips to satin panties!

I had a babysitter growing up who would take me with her if she had an errand to run. I remember a large, black patent leather purse with the handle; a lot of Aqua Net hair spray with dyed, jet black hair teased to God and lilac talcum powder; and a clean, simple dress with a Playtex girdle underneath and tan pantyhose. And her lipstick? A deep, stately pink. That's how she would present herself."

"That does sound nice."

"Even the girdle?" I tease Franklin.

"No comment."

"You don't have to be old to appreciate a certain style of dress or want that style back. I grew up during the 70s and

80s and the tacky things I remember were leg warmers, rainbow suspenders, polyester bell bottoms and weird striped tops, and Jordache jeans. I pray none of those ever come back.

But it was nothing like what you see today. You didn't come to school with skin or booty showing like that. For the life of me, I can't understand why these young girls are wearing yoga pants in schools that don't require a uniform. What downward dog position do *you* plan on doing in math class? Who the hell said you should be comfortable while you learn the periodic table?"

"You know what I miss from that time?" asks Franklin as he gently nudges my head forward to access my neck hairline. "Television shows!"

"Oh, yeah!" I agree with a smile. "I didn't get a tv in my room until I was about 11. I remember The Muppet Show on Sunday nights, followed by…Murder She Wrote, I think? Angela Landsbury is the reason why, to this day, I know that curtains are hung; people are hanged."

"Say what now?" asks Franklin.

"People don't pay attention to when to use hung versus hanged. They say something like…he was hung from a tree. But really they should say the person was *hanged* from a tree."

"And what do they say about a dude who has a big—"

"That's a different context, Franklin," I quickly interrupt, rolling my eyes. "But the shows I really know are the reruns! Get home from school or during summer vacation, turn on Channel 5 or Channel 9 or 11 in New York, you'll see reruns of Get Smart! with Don Adams or Green Acres with Eva Gabor…"

"Did you watch Abbott and Costello movies?" he asks.

"Hell yeah, I did! They showed them on Channel 11 in New York…on Sunday mornings. The Little Rascals showed on Channel 9—"

"The Little Rascals movies was *the* show back then! We loved some Little Rascals. Any time that came on, we sat and watched, man!"

"I really don't understand why people like Mr. Bill Cosby saw that as an embarrassment for black people."

"Hey, don't get me started on Bill Cosby! He lost any rights he had to speak about how black folks should be actin'!" replies Franklin dismissively. "Me, my family, we saw nothin' wrong with the Little Rascals. Buckwheat was smarter than all those little white kids! Brothah always came through and took care of business! Saw things others didn't, was behind the scenes. And all he said was, 'O-kay!' That's it! You knew Buckwheat had your back when he said it!"

"And then you have Stymie—"

"Smooth talkin' brothah man Stymie!" exclaims Franklin. "Got that little hat on his bald head…like a man tryin' to sell you some insurance!"

"To be fair, blacks really should be offended," I say, "because it's totally racist to name a black character after a breakfast cereal, put his hair in pigtails like a pickininny and dress him like a girl. And I've seen racist stuff towards Asians in those movies, too, and the sexist He-Man Woman Hater's Club, swearing off girls.

But I think we don't look at how unusual it was during the *1920s* to make all-kids movies with a diverse cast! You had little girls, blacks, Asians…how else would these filmmakers get away with it unless they catered to racist and sexist stereotypes for laughs? But you had little girls who knew their value, like Darla who didn't put up with any crap from Alfalfa! Homegirl put her man on notice! You wanna get with me? Work for it, honey, 'cause I got a man on standby!"

"Listen, we watched those movies to laugh," says Franklin. "None of us was even think' about racism or any other -isms! We just wanna laugh at a bunch of kids that were smarter than the grown-ups. They put on their little plays and sang, danced and whatnot. Had their clubhouses and secret handshakes. Kids stuff! Not kids in grown-up situations."

"I didn't even think about that! Grown-ups showed up sometimes, but it was all about the children…like Chubbsy-Ubbsy and his crush on Miss Crabtree…Oh, Miss Crabtree! You set my heart aflame!" I finish and Franklin laughs with me. In a wistful tone, I add,

"I doubt you'll see movies like that again."

"Too many child labor laws and political correctness police!" he quips back before leading me to the sinks to wash my hair. During the conditioner, he says above the din of the water spray, "I see your grays have come back."

"Don't remind me. I wish I could just go all gray. I could do something with that."

"I can fix the grays with a color rinse that fades out."

"What color?"

"Red or a cherry red. On your hair you won't really see the color unless you're outside."

"How much extra?"

He tells me the price and I agree to the color rinse. When he's done in the sink, I follow him to his chair. He parts my hair in quarters before snapping on latex gloves. Soon, my hair is covered with a reddish, thick goo. He covers my hair with a plastic cap and sits me under the dryer for 30 minutes. As I'm under the dryer, Franklin finishes the hair of the previous customer.

At the moment when I'm about to doze off, he retrieves me from the dryer and back to the sink, washes out the color rinse and shampoos and conditions my hair a second time. Before I sit in his hair, I check my new hair color in the workstation mirror. I give him my enthusiastic approval. He quickly covers my hair in foam setting lotion. Smoothing and wrapping my hair around my head with a comb and his fingers, he holds the style with wrapping paper, and back I go to the dryer. I see him under the rim of the dryer hood visor take another customer to his chair.

The setting of my hair requires longer time under the dryer, which causes intermittent dozing. The dryer serves as a nice silence chamber from the shop chatter as the barbershop side has a full room of men laughing and talking. As time passes, my head starts to slump; the muffled silence and heat being a good combination for sleep. I jerk awake when Franklin stops the dryer and removes the hood.

Back in his chair, having swapped places with the customer after me, the last leg of my visit begins: The styling.

"You know, speaking of back in the day," I say as he sections my hair and flatirons each piece. "One thing I miss are block parties."

"Yeah…I remember those. We had them a lot in Philly."

"Is that where you've from?"

"Yeah, born and raised," says Franklin. "I still got family there. I remember those summers when the cops would put up barriers so cars couldn't drive through, basically shuttin' down the whole block just for our party. Everybody is cookin' somethin' in their back or front yard, sharing food. Someone brings out their turntable and speakers and plays DJ. Kids riding bikes up and down, don't have to dodge cars. The whole block comin' out. And nothin' bad happened! No shootouts, maybe a little fightin' but nothing serious. And if you were out of line, *anybody* could say somethin' to you about it. Those were nice days, man."

"In my neighborhood, we had ours Labor Day weekend."

"Yup, we did too."

"And my grandmother would buy a whole pig to roast on the barbeque pit in her backyard. She'd have that pig split in half, tied down to the rack, and roast it for 24 hours. The smell of roasting pig would drive you crazy! You wanted to steal a piece, but you were warned not to touch it or you'd get sick," I say with an unexpected smile in remembrance.

"There was always that one person who overcooked their food, though. Shriveled up hot dogs and dried out hamburgers."

"But you took something because it was the polite thing to do to show you appreciated their effort."

"I'd throw mine away when nobody was lookin'," he says.

"I think we all did that at some point. See how polite you were, though? You took that dried up hamburger, said thank you, and threw it away when no one was looking. That's manners *and* civility!"

"Are we gonna start singin' the Archie Bunker theme song now?"

"Wait…I think I remember some of the lyrics," I say, giggling a little before I start to sing a verse from the theme song of the Norman Lear show All in The Family, "Those Were the Days."

"I remember watchin' that when it first came on!" jokes Franklin after he laughs at my Archie and Edith Bunker rendition.

"But I will say that song got one thing right. Back then, girls were girls and men were men. Anything other than that was kept a secret."

"Today everythin' is tumblin' out of closets and if it is in a closet, someone will drag it out real soon!"

"All that foolishness is exhausting, really," I say with a sigh.

"What foolishness?"

"The labels, man, the labels! The labels were simpler growing up and you didn't learn them all until after you graduated high school."

"What labels are you talkin' about?"

"Labels on your sexual identity and sexuality. Nowadays, if I want to tell someone I identify by my birth sex, I say I'm cisgender."

"I thought that was heterosexual," Franklin says.

"No, heterosexual deals with sexual attraction; cisgender deals with sexual identity. Do you identify as a man?"

"Uh…is that a trick question?"

"No, not a trick question. If you're born a male who identifies as male, that makes you cisgender. You have transgender, which means you identify with a gender that's opposite your biological sex, and transsexual means you're transitioning to the sex you identify as, with surgery and hormones. And when you throw sexual attraction into the mix, it gets more complicated."

"Complicated how?" he asks.

"Well, you got asexuality, when you aren't attracted to anyone," I begin. "You have the old standbys: Heterosexuality, bisexuality and homosexuality. Being queer covers attraction and identity related to same sex that doesn't conform to sexuality norms. Then you have pansexuality, when you're attracted to a person rather than their gender—"

"Slow down…what was that now—?"

"And polysexuality," I continue, "which is like bisexuality but it's not because if you're poly, that means you're attracted to the whole shebang…non-binary, hetero and homosexuals, transgender, transsexual—"

"What the hell—?"

"Oh and I forgot non-binary, which means you're…kinda…in between male and female for identity, like an androgynous identity," I explain before finishing with, "And then there's queer *hetero*sexuality, which offends queer people."

"And what's that?"

"Umm…that means…you're attracted to the opposite sex, but you don't follow traditional gender roles in the relationship. Like…the man stays home and does the housekeeping and the woman works. That kind of thing."

"You mean Mr. Mom type stuff."

"I forgot about that movie! Yeah, Mr. Mom! Anyway…with all these labels I could now say, for example, I'm cisgender *and* pansexual, which would tell people I identify as female, my biological sex, and I'm attracted to people and don't care if they're male or female."

"Lemme get this straight," begins Franklin. "I'm cisgender who's heterosexual."

"Yup!" I confirm. "And so am I."

"But I could also be cisgender and homosexual. And if I'm floatin' between being a man and a woman, I'm…transgender—?"

"No. If you float between a male and female identity, you're non-binary. If you're transgender, there's no floating; you've picked a gender opposite your biological sex."

"You mean I've picked a sex," he says.

"No, I don't."

"If I was transgender, I'm pickin' a sex. You just said."

"No, the label clearly says transgender!" I say. "You're *transitioning* to a *gender* that conforms to society's expectations *based* on biological sex. Sex is…is what makes me a woman, it's my ovaries, it's my uterus, it's my—"

"Wait…my bad, that makes me transsexual! That would be me pickin' a sex if I got surgery. But if I was transgender, I'd just be wearin' ladies' clothes and such all the time, but I keep my man parts strapped tight. I get it now."

"Ok, we're back on track," I say.

"And I could be non-binary and homosexual or bisexual."

"Well, I guess, but—"

"Could I be transgender and…what is it?... polysexual?" asks Franklin. "How do you think that works exactly—?"

"Franklin," I interrupt, "there are a lot of combinations that can play out, yes…you could be asexual *and* non-binary! And that's the point I'm trying to make."

"What's the point? I forgot."

"The labels! There are too many of them and if you get one of them wrong, you get labeled ignorant!"

"What sexual identity is that?" asks Franklin.

"Quit playin' with me."

Generation X Dating

"My nerves are shot," I say as I slip into Franklin's chair.

"Uh oh, what's wrong now?" he responds as he drapes a cape around neck.

"I was arguing with my ex-husband. He almost made me late."

"Ex-husband? You jokin' or you got a divorce?"

"No to the first; yes to the second. I'm trying not to advertise it. I still have to deal with him for a few things and he's doing unnecessary passive-aggressive stuff—"

"Ohhhh, I've been there! He's doin' stuff that he knows will piss you off to get you to talk to him," says Franklin.

"Have you been advising my ex-husband?"

Franklin snickers before telling me it's time to reshape my hair style. I am on the fence about cutting it because I like the growth so far; nevertheless, I agree to the reshaping with no use of the clippers. He grabs his scissors from his workstation and begins to cut my dirty hair.

"To answer your question," Franklin continues, "I have *not* been *advising* your ex-husband. I guessed from experience."

"As the person receiving or giving?"

"Both. And not just in my marriages. With any breakup there's always gonna be that person that can't accept that things are over."

"Is that what's going on with my ex? He can't accept that fact that a marriage he didn't really want is over?"

"Hey, I ain't in the man's head!" he says with a laugh. "All I can tell you is that from my experience, if a person is doin' stuff that they know will make you react, they'll keep doin' it. They might be tryin' to make you angry so you'll talk to 'em. Even if you two are screamin' at each other. That kind of attention is better than no attention for some people."

"All I know is that it's exhausting. Each time he tries something, I'm like, you don't have to act this way. You don't have to be like this. You can stop what you're doing at any time. We both agreed to the divorce…contract terminated!"

"No argument," replies Franklin. "We can sit here and make it sound like it's so easy and simple for people in a broken relationship to just end things and move on. But for some men and women, it ain't that simple. They got issues from the past and now they got a new issue to add to the old ones."

"Well, I *was* his second marriage," I concede.

"See? He's probably got issues from that marriage."

"And they came tumbling out during ours."

"It sometimes works out that way. We all come into relationships with baggage. Some are better at hidin' it than others. For a long time, too!" Franklin ends with a laugh.

"The trouble is the person who's doing the hiding is sending out signals the other person ignores or excuses. There were signs of that baggage while we were dating, but I excused them like I was being gaslighted. 'No, he didn't say what I think he just said. I'm looking too much into it.' You know that rationalization that goes on," I say.

"Do I! Man, everything is sweet and happy at the beginning, ain't it? You two are diggin' on each other, holdin' hands, talkin' until late at night over the phone. And then suddenly the cracks show…she starts doin' things…small stuff at first—"

"And you don't pay close attention to it. Because you're still in that sweetheart phase of things—"

"The cracks get wider and before you know it, you got a crater in your backyard and no clue how it got there!" counters Franklin.

"And all because that person thought those issues weren't really issues, just peccadillos," I say.

"Pecca-what?"

"Peccadillos! It means…a petty sin or trifling fault. One of my favorite words. Plus, it's fun to say."

"Yeah, it is kinda fun to say," says Franklin after muttering the word a few more times under his breath. "And it means what again?"

"A petty sin or a trifling fault," I repeat with a smile. "We all have peccadillos."

"Some more than others."

"Anyway, all these changes in dating are exhausting…it makes you not want to try again."

"Marriage too?" he asks.

"I dunno. I'll admit I've participated in online dating from when it became a thing in the late '90s. As a matter of fact, that's how I met my ex, dressing up to meet some random guy I liked on a profile who I hope didn't kill me. And now, here I am doing it all over again, swiping right on guys who have pics of *things* instead of their face. Or guys holding a dead fish in the air. This one guy had a profile saying he caught his wife cheating and he's lonely because he's getting a divorce and just wants a 'one-night'."

"One night of what?"

"I think he meant one night stand and got lazy."

"Now you gotta advertise for a one night, huh?" snorts Franklin. "Back in the days you went to the club for that. Buy a lady a drink, dance a little and if your game was on point, she'd go home with you," Franklin says, sounding wistful.

"At lease in the club you have a lesser chance of being catfished—"

"Catfished? Is that still a thing? I thought that tv show killed all that."

"Not completely. Apparently, in the online dating world today, my age makes me a target for romance scammers. They have articles about it in AARP, which makes me feel ever older! I look at all my profiles to figure out what exactly is there that makes them think that I'm a good target."

"You already said it! Your age!" replies Franklin. "These scammers figure you got kids out of the house; you lonely and you got extra money to give up for a little company, some lovin' attention. This game ain't new; they just moved it online. There were pimps and playahs that played house with these older women way back when! That money…and home cooked food! got took with a kiss and a smile."

"And they're so devious with it, stealing pics from some hot guy's profile and passing themselves off as that person. If I was just as devious as they are, I'd trap all of them with a fake profile and then shut them down! That would give me great satisfaction."

"You ever got took?" asks Franklin.

"Almost. I'll admit it," I say. "The game was good, and then I started thinking the game was too good, you know? He said all the right things, had an answer for everything. Then he made his first ask for money and that's when I started looking at the pics he kept sharing. Next thing you know, I'm on the internet looking for images and I find out the dude is as fake as a $3 bill. I even contacted the real person through social media to let him know his pics were being used in a romance scam."

"Why'd you do all that?"

"Because I hate a liar and I hate being took by one. I felt in control when I did it. And then you have the guys advertising for a FWB because they're in a sexless marriage, so you only see shots of their crotch—"

"A…FWB?" interrupts Franklin. "What's that again? I forgot."

"Friends with benefits," I reply, "you know, a series of hookups with one person and no commitment."

"Where does the friends part fit in?"

"It doesn't!" I say with a chuckle. "When Harry Met Sally already proved men and women can't be friends! I think they put in that word to make it sound better. I find the phrase deceptive. There's no friendship! What happens if the sex is bad? Is it still a benefit?"

"I met my women the old school way. On a street corner."

"Even your current wife?"

"Naw, I met her through a friend of mine."

"You were lucky," I say. "But it's not that easy, at least for me. I wouldn't want anyone I know trying to fix me up with someone."

"Why not? What's wrong with that?" he asks.

"Because my approximation of good looking may be different from theirs."

"So, it's all about looks, huh?"

"No, it's not," I say. "People perceive things differently, especially what makes a person attractive. There are guys I've liked who weren't pretty boys, but there was something about them…it may be his eyes or his teeth or his—"

"His teeth?"

"Yeah, I'm a sucker for a cute smile and the teeth gotta be even! Unless they're a toddler."

"Ok, I get you," says Franklin. "Continue."

"That's why I don't want someone going through the trouble to hook me up with someone who will ultimately disappointment me," I say.

"I don't understand all this dating difficulty," Franklin says as he brushes the remnants of my hair off my cape. "When I was young, things were simple. You hangin' out with your boys, a cute girl walks by, you try to get her attention and if she responds, you walk with her until you get that number!"

"No, no, you can't do that today. There's no 'excuse me, miss, can I get your number?' Those days are over, especially for my age range."

"Then how else are you gonna meet people?" he asks.

"There you go! You finally get it. I don't want to go to church just to meet a guy, that's…weird and wrong. I don't like bars; a bunch of hot, sweaty, liquored up people looking for a hit-it-and-quit it. So, I set up profiles on multiple dating apps and hope someone decent responds. Believe it or not, I kinda agree with you on the old school way of meeting guys…just walking down the street, you catch someone's eye, and then suddenly you hear, 'excuse me, miss? Can I talk at you for a second?'"

"Yeeeeaaaaah!" Franklin shouts joyously and I laugh.

This appointment was a simple one, just a trim and style. Franklin goes though the regular motions to get my hair clean and conditioned. Then he slicks my hair to my head with foam styling lotion and sends me back under the dryer. Forty-five minutes later I'm back in his chair and I say,

"There's something else I noticed that's changed in dating now."

"What is that?"

"The color lines and age limits in dating have disappeared a little bit," I continue. "I'm hearing more from white men my age and younger than from black men. The young ones mostly. Suddenly, *mature women* are a thing and it's so obvious they're working out mommy issues and secret fantasies. Some profiles say straight out they're lying about their age because they want an older woman and I'm like…what new kind of foolishness is this? It makes me wonder what other issues they're working out with an older black woman."

"So have you?" asks Franklin.

"Have I what?"

"Dated a young white guy."

"I wouldn't call what we did a date, per se—"

"Oh, so it was a FWB thing?" jokes Franklin.

"No, no. They, these young people, don't call it a date. They call it 'hanging out,' which means we go somewhere basic and I wind up paying for shit because they make $15 an hour. Besides, I'm conflicted when I consider dating outside my race, especially a white guy."

"Can't handle that guilt, huh?" jokes Franklin.

"I do feel guilt. I'll admit it," I reply. "I should be past all of that today, you know? But I grew up during the old New York City days of Howard Beach and Tawana Brawley and Public Enemy. I grew up on subliminal messages that say by every black man's side should be a strong black woman. Think about tv shows like Good Times and The Jefferson…Alex Haley's Roots! Look at what happened to

O.J. Simpson! If that ain't a cautionary tale, then I don't know what is! If I say I only date black men, does that make me a racist? If I only date white men, does it mean I hate my black men?"

"Don't think too hard on that," says Franklin. "We all got preferences for who we wanna get with, ok? I love every flavah of black woman out there! From your butter pecan to dark chocolate chip! I love my sistahs. Ya'll can be crazy as hell at times, but God made you from man so we can't complain too much! That's my *preference* 'cause I feel most comfortable around them. If you wanna date black men 'cause you think a black man will understand you better, ain't nothin' wrong with that! But if you're lookin' for certain qualities in a man and he happens to be white or whatever and that person gets you, ain't nothin' wrong with that either."

"Soooo, what are you saying?"

"What I'm sayin' is havin' a preference don't make you racist or a hater. You wanna date spicy papìs? You want a vanilla donut stick dunked in your coffee? Some chai in your tea? That's your business and nobody else's."

"Some *chai* in my *tea*?" I repeat, laughing along with him. "And what about you?"

"What about me?"

"Have you ever crossed the color line?"

"Nope! Not me! Ain't never messed with white chicks. I've *seen things* that make me stay away from that's line…don't even toe that line. Too much stress in datin' white women."

"So, you have crossed that line?"

"No! I said I seen things…didn't say that stuff happened to me. Now let me think…," Franklin begins as he tilts my head to the side. "I think I was still living in Philly at the time…yeah, I was maybe about…24? There's this dude from around the way and he was seein' this white chick who couldn't stay out of the 'hood…she loved the brothahs! She was the type that thought she was black 'cause she hung out with black folks…you know what I mean."

"Like a caricature of what a black woman is supposed to be."

"Exactly that! And everybody warned this dude to stay away from her 'cause she's trouble, but he don't listen! He was hard-headed to begin with, always in trouble for petty stuff here and there. Before he was with the white chick, he was with his baby's mama—"

"Was she black?" I ask.

"Yeah, she was black. Anyway, they broke up, but not really. It was their thing…they'd break up to make up. But this time, things are different and he hooks up with this white chick when before, he'd be messin' around with…Delphine down the way, you know, or Delphine's sister! But he ain't never messed around with a white woman before, least of all the one everybody warned him about.

So, he's with the white chick, but things don't stay sweet and sunny! He had been tryin' to keep things secret so his baby's mama didn't find out. Why? 'Cause they had got back together; he was seein' both women at the same time! But like I said, he's a knucklehead and he wasn't smart enough to hold up that situation forever 'cause people talk!

One day my mom asked me to run an errand for her… I think I had to pick up somethin' from my aunt's house. At the time I had this old Dodge Dart, a four-door that you could hear from blocks away that my uncle gave me. He said if I could get it to run, it was mine. It wasn't much, but it got me where I needed to go. And on that day, I just so happened to pass by his place on the way to my aunt's house and there I see him and three women yellin' and screamin' at each other."

"Three women?"

"Yeah! The white chick, his baby's mama and her sister."

"The cat was out of the bag, huh?"

"Man, everythin' was outta the bag that day! I double park and go over 'cause I knew his baby's mama, I knew her family and they don't play! And man! that girl could cuss. There she is with a big ole belly callin' that white girl all kinds of names…him too! My mom knew her, always said her mouth should be washed out with soap!"

"I knew a girl in my neighborhood like that," says Tasha, Franklin's workstation compadre. "She was this tiny little thing and had a mouth like a trucker! Now, I'm for using a cuss word or two, but she took it to a new level! She was pregnant and everyone said that baby gonna pop out cussin' his momma for takin' so long!"

Those who hear the comment, including me, burst out in laughter and when it subsides, finally catching on to what he said earlier, I say to Franklin, "Wait…she was pregnant with his child? Oh, that dirty dog!"

"Yeah, man! Pregnant or no, she was gonna beat down that white chick! There he is, tryin' to keep them apart and he's losin' the battle. Just then, the white chick says somethin'…I can't remember what, and the sister starts chargin' for her! I was quick enough to pull her away. By this time, the whole neighborhood is watchin' this and *nobody*'s steppin' in to stop it! Just standin' there laughin' and talkin'. I could see if that if I let this go on, someone was goin' to lockup and it sure wasn't gonna be the white chick, especially in those days."

"Sounds like a Jerry Springer episode. And then what happened?"

"I started cussin' at all of them and reminded them of what I just told you…if they continue with this, the cops are gonna show up and one of us *black folks* is goin' to jail tonight all over some white woman…and I pointed at her…who has no business in the 'hood! Then the white chicks starts yellin' at me 'cause she don't like what I said…and then the arguin' starts all over again."

"You were done by then, huh?"

"I was *more* than done…I was *overdone*! So, I grab the baby mama and the sister and I tell them I'm takin' them home right now. Then I tell the white woman to go back where she came from, no need to stay around 'cause you just found out you were the side chick, not the main chick, so go find some other black man to destroy! I warned her the baby mama got family, cousins all over Philly, so watch herself!"

"Tryin' the scare her out of the 'hood?"

"No, that really was a warnin'. That family is large…ten brothers and sisters and all of 'em got children all over Philly.

Cousins on top of cousins and they crazy as hell," says Franklin.

"What happened to the guy? You still keep in touch?"

"Nah, we weren't that tight to stay in touch. But I did hear he finally married his baby's mama, though."

"Was it right after what happened with the white chick?" I ask.

"Ummm…maybe a few years later? Maybe longer. I think that whole situation smartened him up."

"See? That's another reason why you gotta be careful about the people you *hook up* with" I say. "You might wind up with a fatal attraction or even worse! There's too many STDs out there. Did you know syphilis and chlamydia have made a comeback? Of all the diseases to come back, it had to be those two! AIDS cases on the rise…again. And I'm like, damn! I thought we had that under control for a minute."

"Or so you thought. Just 'cause it ain't in the news, don't mean it still ain't happenin'."

"True. But it goes beyond just catching an STD, though," I say.

"Goes beyond? How?"

"Well, at the heart of all of those STDs is dishonesty."

"Dishonesty?" asks Franklin.

"Yeah, hear me out for a second. I get that people may not always know if they're carrying an STD until the symptoms show. But sometimes people see the signs and ignore them and *dishonestly* pass what they have to their partner, or their one-night stand."

"I agree with you there," says Franklin. "I've been burned a few times from women who knew their kitty cat was on fire."

"It's reckless! How can you sleep with multiple partners, in many cases with no protection, and not expect to catch some sort of disease? You rarely hear someone say, 'I get tested regularly and I screen my one-night stands before I sleep with them.' This is the 21st century, not Ancient Rome! But people are people. And it should be no surprise that kind of behavior has consequences if you're not *honest* with yourself.

I'm not sayin' you can't sleep around; if you wanna call that embracing your sexuality, you wanna raise the flag of feminism, well, ok, whatever! But stop lying to yourself that you couldn't possibly catch a disease. You better have a year's stash of condoms if you don't care about the sexual history. And now there's this…ethical creeping movement happening where you can date and sleep with others as long as everyone agrees."

"That kind of stuff…the ethical creepin' you call it, that's a new thing with these young people," replies Franklin. "But folks in my age range, in your age range, we weren't raised to do all that negotiatin' to be with other people! If us men wanted a side piece, we did it the way it's been done since Jesus was a boy…behind that woman's back!"

"I think that's the point of disclosing you're seeing other people," I say. "See what happened with your boy in Philly? Sneaking around and got caught...violence! Disclosure eliminates the stress of someone's feelings getting hurt and keep everything from turning into a hot mess express…everybody knows the deal, so don't catch feelings because it ain't on the menu!"

"Eliminate stress? Says who? I ain't never met a woman who'd agree to me gettin' some sexual healin' or anythin' else from another woman! If she do, she either don't care 'cause she got her own side piece or she ain't all that good lookin'!"

"I'll forget you just said that."

"Sometimes the truth ain't pretty!" says Franklin before singing a verse of the old '60s Jimmy Soul song "If You Wanna Be Happy," emphasizing the last line of the verse, "get an ugly girl to marry you!"

I chastise him when he's done with his singing and, picking up the conversation where I left off, I say, "I've read message boards chatting for and against that setup. Yet, I feel like the ones who want it are on this agenda to show everybody how wonderful it is…like, hey! You too can enjoy ethical dating with multiple partners for the low, low price of $19.99!

But we don't see the follow up, do we? At the time they wrote those praises, things were probably working and everybody was happy, happy, happy! Are things still working? Or did the baggage of past relationships pile up too high? All you need is one person in that whole convoluted situation to be in denial about what they really want…and it all comes tumbling down like Jenga."

"My grandma used to say houses with bad foundations will crumble to the ground," says Franklin.

The Decline of English Language

Summer has finally arrived; temperatures are consistent and with that comes an unexpected hiccough that often happens in the lives of working-class people only this time it happens to me: unemployment. When you don't have a full-time job with full time pay, sacrifices must be made. This means the squeakiest wheel gets the most grease and luxuries such as going to a hairdresser or a nail salon for a little bit of beauty are the things that are sacrificed. In the meantime, I attempt a few of Franklin's methods, which include cutting my hair lopsided using a multitude of mirrors, and applying drug store relaxers that leave my hair dry and fried. Determined to right my hair care wrongs, I rob Peter to pay Paul and make an appointment with Franklin, justifying this luxury as a well-earned treat for scoring a temporary, six-month contract for work after two months of unemployment.

Franklin has moved his base of operations again, ironically next door to my nail salon. This location doesn't share a space with a barbershop like the last one; it's a long space of workstations with wall mirrors, salon chairs, hair dryers, sinks and ladies of various ages, with Franklin in his regular role as the rooster of the hen house.

However, when I sit in Franklin's chair this time, I sense a little awkwardness from him in this new environment. The shop's owner, Nona, a buxom, older black woman with short, spiky hair dyed a bright cherry red, works directly across from him, which gives her a bird's eye view of his styling technique. This was new for us; at his past location the shop owner wasn't present for my appointments. We engage in some pleasantries before he springs a question on me that he's never sprung before:

"You ever tried a finger wave?"

"You mean like a…a…Betty Boop, Josephine Baker-type finger wave?"

"Yeah."

"No. Do *you* think that's a good look for me?"

"I dunno. Willing to try?"

I get the sense that Franklin is trying to impress the other beauticians with his sweet styling skills and to prove he belongs there, so I reluctantly agree to the experiment. He tut-tuts me for the state of my hair and immediately grabs the scissors to cut.

Lowering my voice I ask, "So…uh…why the new location? What was wrong with the last one?"

With his voice equally low, he responds, "Man, I had to leave that place. There was fightin' and whatnot goin' on. I had to step in one time…two dudes started swingin' at each other for somethin' stupid! I had to hold the dude back! Someone wanted to call the police…customers all upset…had children there. Right after that I started looking for a new place. This is closer to home than the other place."

"Well, thank you for finding a place next door to my nail salon."

"You know me, I aim to please!"

Right then, my phone vibrates and I check for a message from one of my sons.

"Oh, for heaven's sake!" I mutter as I type a response.

"Everythin' alright?"

"Yeah, everything's fine. My son is so lazy with his texting. All these damn acronyms…and he uses them as though I should know what he's saying. I have to take extra time to ask what does that mean? How's that for making someone feel ancient?"

"That happens with every generation."

"True. There was slang in the '80s…that's dope! She's fly! Word to the mothah! Broke as a joke! And the rap scene is where we learned most of that vocabulary. But those were…words! Our acronyms were simpler and made sense! ASAP! PDQ! Now we got ridiculous acronyms like 'LOL,' for example. Why do we need an acronym to tell the other person you thought what they said was funny? Have we gotten so lazy that we can't just say 'funny!' and leave it at that? You wanna shorten that too? How about 'ha,' which is even *shorter* than LOL!"

"One of my kids texted…what was it?…TBH! and I thought he just typed TBS the tv channel wrong. I'm tryin' to play it cool, thinkin' I understood it…and three lines into the conversation my son says, 'Pop, TBH means to be honest.' I never felt so stupid in my life!"

"I think that's why these abbreviations were created! To make old people like you and me feel stupid. Guess what else? LOL is in the dictionary!" I say.

"Say what now?"

To prove my point, I pull out my phone and search for the term in the online Merriam Webster dictionary to show him the proof.

"Would you look at that!" he exclaims as he reads the screen. "LOL…abbreviation…laugh out loud; laugh-*ing* out loud! We need that explanation in a dictionary, huh?"

"Apparently," I reply, pulling away the phone. "Along with TBH, LMAO—"

"Hold up a minute! They got LMAO in the dictionary?"

"Yes, but not LMFAO! Makes no sense! Fuck is in the dictionary, so if you've got LMAO, why not LMFAO? Doesn't *that* need clarification? And why did Merriam Webster leave out RFLO but Cambridge Dictionary didn't?"

"How you know all that?" asks Franklin.

"Because someone used it on me and I looked it up so I wouldn't sound stupid when I responded."

"What is it?"

"Rolling on the floor laughing out loud," I reply with a little laugh. "Saying it out loud I can see why that would be an acronym; it's a mouthful."

"What's the difference between LMFAO and RFLO?"

"I have no idea! One is maybe the cleaner version of the other? For those who don't like cuss words in their acronyms. Or religious people…you know…I guess that would be in heavy rotation among holy and sanctified."

"But how would people know the 'F' in RFLO stands for floor?" says Franklin who suddenly stops cutting. "And why isn't there an extra 'L' in RFLO? It should be RFLOL," Franklin asks.

"It is! but in the Cambridge Dictionary, the 'L' is missing," is my reply.

"Who makes up this stuff? Like, who decides what goes in a dictionary? Is there, I dunno, a vote for a word? Do the public get to say anythin' about it?"

"That's a good question! No idea. I imagine a room full of white men with receding hairlines, half-glasses on hawk noses, thin lips twisted in a permanent scowl calling the shots."

"What about those…emojis? Don't need acronyms if we use those," comments Franklin.

"No, we don't! They're definitely quicker and more accurate. But even the use of emojis is getting out of hand—"

"Oh yeah…my wife told me what a peach and eggplant mean. Never would've guessed that one."

"Who would guess veggies and fruits would be used to mean body parts? I sure didn't!" I say.

"What about the kitty cat emoji? Does that stand for—?"

"No! That's the taco emoji," I clarify.

"So, the eggplant stands for—"

"Yep!" I say.

"And the peach and taco emojis stand for—"

"Yeah! Isn't that weird?" I say. "The peanuts emoji needs no explanation. You pair any of those with the sweat or tongue hanging out emoji and you have pictographic porn.

No needs for words of seduction…just tongue, sweat and eggplant emojis. The millennials thought all that up."

"Have you used them, young lady?" Franklin asks teasingly.

"Never have I ever used food emojis for sexting. I'm a big girl…I know how to use my words."

Franklin laughs as he leads me from the chair to the back of the parlor to shampoo and condition my hair. So deep was I in our conversation that I forgot about the hairdo I had committed to at the beginning: finger waves. With my hair still damp, he begins to apply the sculpting gel with the spine of a rat tail comb, creating flapper girl-type waves that start from my widow's peak. From the first wave I know I'll wind up washing out this effort the minute I get home. My odd-shaped head was not meant for swirls of stiff hair plastered to my scalp. For a few hours I'll just have to look like my grandmother with a fresh hairdo for church.

"You know who I think is conspiring to ruin English?" I say suddenly. "The millennials."

"Conspirin'? Sounds dramatic," he says.

"Ok then, do you know what suss means?"

"Suss…suss," Franklin repeats as though he's trying to guess the origin of the word. A beat later, he says, "Suspect? Suspicious?"

"Yep! And slay?"

"I'm guessin' it don't mean with the jawbone of an ass," comments Franklin as he starts waving a new section of hair.

"It means you did well. And for the life of me, I don't know how bae, a Scandinavian word for poop, wound up being used to describe someone you're dating or someone you like."

"Feels recycled," he says.

"Doesn't it though? If you look at these millennial terms, some were used in the 70s and 80s. Like…bet! I said bet all the time in high school. Or boujee."

"Us black folks been usin' boujee for a while!" declares Franklin. "So, basically these kids are takin' somethin' old and makin' it new again."

"You got it! Some words made the cut by millennials as worthy, others didn't. The more these words get shortened, the more our vocabulary bank shrinks and we're unable to say words that are more than one syllable. A slippery slope to an idiocracy," I conclude.

"Like song lyrics today!" exclaims Franklin. "They dumb down these lyrics so much a two-year-old can sing 'em! Ten-year-olds runnin' around singin' too-grown lyrics 'cause their parents or their auntie or cousin is blastin' that junk throughout the house. I grew up on songs with great lyrics…grown folks lyrics that you don't sing until you can understand what they mean! Teddy Pendagrass, Marvin Gaye, Eddie Kendricks, Betty Wright, Patti LaBelle and the Bluebells, Stevie Wonder, The O'Jays…whooo! These groups had lyrics you could feel right down to your socks!"

"Like the song 'If You Don't Know Me by Now'?"

"Teddy Pendagrass had Philly proud! You could count on that song played at every cookout, every house party, in every car. Teddy was one of the great ones, may he rest in peace."

"I think my favorite Marvin Gaye song is 'Inner City Blues'. Those lyrics are timeless! That's the mark of a good songwriter in my opinion, one who can write a song that's powerful and relevant 30, 40, 50 years from now," I say.

"That's everybody's favorite! I like Marvin in his Tami Terrell days…I remember dancin' with a girl at a birthday party to 'You're All I Need to Get By.' Man, those were good days!"

"My mother used to listen to WBLS FM in New York with Hal Jackson. She played it on an old clock radio she kept in the kitchen. I remember hearing 'I Love Music' and 'Back Stabbers' on that radio."

"Now that song, 'Back Stabbers,' had timeless lyrics!" exclaims Franklin gleefully before singing a verse to The O'Jays' song, sounding surprisingly close to Gerald LaVert.

"Beautiful!" I say as everyone claps at the impromptu performance. "Hearing you sing it makes me realize who The O'Jays could've been talking about when they say some of your buddies look shady."

"Who?" he asks.

"Julius Cesar! It's a warning to watch his back on those senate steps. The Ides of March, they call it. Think about it…blades clenched tight in their fist—"

"And the lady they was out to get was Cleopatra!" Franklin enthusiastically agrees. "Never paid attention to the lyrics like that before! We got back stabbers today, don't we?"

"We sure do! Those lyrics are almost like a parable if you think about it. No three-year-old is gonna embarrass you at grandma's during Thanksgiving if they sing it! They may be grown folks' lyrics, but there's nothing in there for shock value.

I remember when Vanity 6's 'Nasty Girl' song first came out. To this day, everyone remembers how nasty that song really was for that time! Most of my generation…we were teenagers when that song came out and we were like…yooo! That's Eddie Murphy raw right there! If we repeated those lyrics and started gyrating like Vanity 6…you got a definite smack in the mouth! And we never thought the lyrics changed feminism forever…because it didn't! It was just another song produced by Prince!

But with a Marvin… or a Teddy or an O'Jay's song, I think people will always agree the lyrics from these singers can move you…and they speak to you regardless of the time you're listening to them. I'm not saying just those cats pumped out good music…we got young artists now taking what those guys did and carrying the torch of timeless music.

How many times were you in the supermarket…and an O'Jay's song comes on? What do you start doing? You start that cute, little side-to-side shuffle dance because you're transported to your backyard birthday party or somebody's wedding. You can play those songs at any protest, put them in any documentary, use them to motivate people. It's called soul music for a reason."

"I get your point," says Franklin. "But the 'Nasty Girl' song did touch me, though."

"But it wasn't your soul, was it?"

"Nope."

Love and Marriage

It's rare that I'm invited to a gala event. The company I contract with is having a formal dress fundraising event and I take that opportunity to treat myself to a makeover that includes hair, nails and a makeup session at my go-to department store makeup counter, and wearing my gently worn halter dress that's a beautiful, satiny aubergine color that makes me feel like royalty.

Franklin's chair is the first stop on my day of beauty. I tell him about my special event, which will occur in the evening, and he assures me all is well in his capable hands. Knowing my nail appointment immediately follows this visit, he gets to work, starting with a haircut.

"Goin' through a lot of trouble for all this glamour," Franklin says after a moment of silence.

"Is there a question in there?"

"Gettin' dolled up for a special someone?"

"Nope."

"You ain't takin' anybody? No dressed-up man on your arm?"

"Nope!"

"Dressed-up woman? If that's your thing…"

"The only two women who can flip me to the other side of the fence are Padma Lakshmi and Selma Hayek.

Otherwise, I ride that pony…there's always a saddle waiting!" I reply jokingly.

"Jump on it!" Franklin jokes along with me, laughing.

"I am doing all of this…glamourizing because I wanna feel pretty tonight and for no other reason!"

After a beat, Franklin mutters, "You might meet someone there, you never know."

I sigh before saying, "I'm not interested in anyone right now. Dating today has gotten so convoluted. I'm fine flying solo for a while. Some people can bounce back quickly after a divorce and I'm not one of those people."

"I get that. I think men bounce back quicker than women," he says.

"You've noticed that too, huh? My ex-husband had someone waiting in the wings. He went straight from me to his va-jay-jay upgrade, which really wasn't much of an upgrade; I've seen what she looks like."

"He was cheatin' on you, huh?"

"Yes…no…maybe…I don't know. I have no real proof that he was cheating on me while we were married, but everything pointed in that direction. It doesn't really matter anymore. It's over. I need to be by myself for a while, maybe a very long while."

"What? You gonna keep everything all lock up? Let cobwebs grow down there?"

When I'm done snickering at his joke, I reply, "No, I don't mean it that way. I just need to stretch out and see who I am on my own. I was married for six years, trying to be someone's wife and now I need to get used to things, like, having the bed to myself. I still sleep on 'my side' of the bed and when you do that, it reminds you that the person you shared a space with day and night is no longer there. And that…empty space might tempt you into unhealthy relationships just to fill it."

"I never thought about it that deeply. When I got divorced…*three times!*…I felt bad and miserable, don't get me wrong, but I didn't think about the empty side of beds and whatnot."

"Men only think about those things if a spouse passes away."

"No, not all men are like that! Stop stereotyping us! There are men like me who feel bad about how things went down, but we aren't lookin' at how we sleep in our bed."

"I'll tell you one thing", I say. "All the stars need to be in alignment before I say 'I do' again. And honestly, I don't understand why gay people fought for the right to get married."

"Hey! I'm not plugged in to most of the stuff that's goin' on these days, but I do understand why they did!"

"Oh, yes, it's about equality, isn't it?" I say, restraining the sarcastic tone I want to use.

"You don't think it was about that, huh?" asks Franklin. "Then what exactly?"

"On the face of things, it was about equality, the right to do the same things as heterosexual couples and be recognized by the government. But guess what it also does? Gives you the right to have your divorce recognized, too!

Break it down even more and not only have they fought for the right to have the government recognize their marriage, they also fought for the right to ask the government for permission to end that marriage. You've been to divorce court; I've been to divorce court…your marriage ain't over until the court says it is. The narrative about gay marriage doesn't mention that nasty aspect of sharing your life with someone…as though the possibility of divorce couldn't possibly happen for people who fought for that right. But it does happen and I wish people wouldn't pretend it doesn't. People are people, gay or straight, relationships fall apart, and pain follows. Fighting for the right to marry means you want your failing relationship on display and part of official record."

"Lemme ask you a question."

"Shoot," I say.

"When you got married, did you ever think you'd get divorced?"

"No, of course not."

"Right, no one says 'I do, but we won't be together for long.'," says Franklin. "All you have in your head is that you love that person and you wanna share your life with 'em. You takin' a big chance. Maybe that's what they were fightin' for, that chance to fail in a relationship just like straight people do and have it be seen as just as good."

"Do you need the government to witness it or give you permission to have it, though?" I reply. "People who don't get married fail at relationships every damn day and the government knows nothing about them. And when they fail, the couple makes the decision to split assets and say good-bye forever…not a judge. On top of all that, you have to ask the government to get your name back, the name you're born with! In some states, you have to go to probate court to get it back if you don't declare it at the time you divorce…probate court! The court that handles your assets when you die!"

"Oh damn! I didn't know that," he says with surprise in his voice. "Come to think of it, I never asked my ex-wives how they did it."

"You know why you didn't know that? Because in the past a name change affected only who? Women! Do you know the hassle in changing your name back on your social security card, driver's license, at your job so they can change tax withholding and insurance…even your damn mortgage! I couldn't even change the name on the title for my house without having to produce my divorce papers and do what? Pay a fee! This is what gay people fought for…well, good luck with all that."

"And if there's a lot of money involved…that can make things even more messy," adds Franklin.

"It's funny you mention that. The court case that started it all was about money…or rather the right to inherit money from a romantic partner you've lived with and not have it taxed to death. Our country's tax structure was initially set up to encourage heterosexual marriage, I won't deny that, but…look at the tax rules! You get a discount on how much money you pay back to the government if you file married jointly, but you pay more if you file married but separate, or you're single."

"That's true," concedes Franklin. "I had our tax man break it down for me 'cause it made no sense to me. That's why young single folks are strugglin', havin' to pay all that tax."

"Meanwhile, you have people on Medicaid who are penalized if they get married because you need to be dead ass broke to be on Medicaid and combining income that's probably $22,000 a year between the two of them puts them over the threshold for keeping their benefits. How messed up is that? A 70- or 80-year-old meets that special someone they want to live out the rest of their days with…guess what? They can't marry because they'll lose their benefits…for wanting to honor a marriage system that's been ingrained in them since they were a child. The government will penalize them because they weren't able to pay into the system…they were poor, disabled, whatever. For those who pay and play by the man's rules, you're rewarded. For those who didn't, they're punished by dangling, out of reach, the right for that union to be recognized," I finish.

"Me and wife discussed that before we got married. I pay my payroll taxes on my income, but with me being older than her, we need to keep an eye on that business."

"Yes, keep on top of that. If you paid 10 years of payroll taxes, you'd be on Medicare and having a spouse affects your benefits. The tax laws in this country will never change because there's more incentive to keep the status quo. I would rather have a common law marriage with powers of attorney for important stuff, like…catastrophic illness or something. I set up a trust, a living will…bam! Everything that can be covered is. And if it isn't, it won't matter to me because I'll be either incapacitated or dead."

"Man, you sure know how to suck all the fun outta romance!"

"We weren't talking about romance," I say. "We were talking about marriage!"

"Romance leads to marriage."

"No, love leads to marriage. Frank Sinatra said so. Love *and* marriage, love *and* marriage!"

"All he's sayin' is that they go together. He ain't sayin' one leads to the other," Franklin argues.

"But it stands to reason that one leads to the other," I reply. "You're sharp at this time of day, ain't you?"

"Like a Ginsu knife. I'm a morning person."

Once he's finished his cut, he leads me to the sink for a shampoo and conditioner. When I'm back in his chair, he makes final tweaks to his cut and then applies foam setting lotion, taking a moment beforehand to decide which direction he wants my hair to set. An hour later, my hair slick and bone dry, I'm in his chair and he's massaging hair oil into my scalp.

"If I do get married again," I say as Franklin begins to curl my hair. "I won't share a bed with my husband. I want my own bedroom."

"If I tried sellin' that idea to my wife, she'd have all kinds of thoughts goin' through her head," comments Franklin. "Why you need your own bedroom? You don't like sleepin' with me? What's wrong with me?"

"See how brainwashed we are about what it means to live with someone we've partnered with?" I ask. "Why do we have to share *everything*? Does our privacy stop because we have someone in our lives sharing the same space? I mean, hey, I love you, I know you love me, but why does that mean I have to share body heat with you every night of our lives? Who said I have to constantly clean your pubic hair off our shared toilet? Why should living in a separate room means I love you less?"

"You tryin' to make this simple, but you ain't thinkin' about how fragile you women are!" says Franklin.

"Excuse me?"

"You know what I mean. If you want me to say insecure, then I'll say it. You women are insecure! If a man went to his wife and said, 'hey, baby, let's sleep in separate rooms,' what do you think would be the first thought in her head? Do you think it's gonna be, 'Finally! He…uh…said it before I could!'? Hell naw! Her first thought is gonna be, 'Huh? Why he want that all of a sudden? What's he up to?' Tell me I'm wrong!"

My response is a sigh and he starts cackling.

"That insecurity can go both ways, you know. With some men," I counter.

"I'm not sayin' men ain't insecure. But if a wife went to her husband with that, at first the man might think some things…but he'll slide into the idea more quickly than a woman would because you know what that means? He don't have to fight for room in the closet! He don't have to hear complaints about how hot he's makin' the bed! He don't have to fight for the covers! He can fart as much as he wants! He don't have someone pokin' him awake when all he wants to do is sleep! He can watch whatever he wants on that bedroom tv! Everythin' you women consider disgustin' we can now do it in peace! Plus, we don't have to perform when we really don't want to!"

By this time, I'm doubled over in the chair, laughing and gasping for air.

"Thank you for supporting my requirement of separate bedrooms!" I manage to say when my laughter subsides.

"So, you can talk about brainwashin' and whatnot," Franklin says as he resumes styling my hair, "but it ain't about what we've been conditioned to do. Like you said, people are people and they're used to things being a certain way."

"You know who Frida Kahlo was?"

"She's that painter, ain't she? From Mexico? The one eyebrow."

"That's the one. Anyway, she was married to another Mexican painter, Diego Garcia. During their marriage they lived in separate houses connected by a bridge."

"Separate houses? That's an invitation for trouble," says Franklin.

"It kinda was in their case. He wound up sleeping with Frida's sister. She caught them one day on a visit. They're a bad example…ignore that… but living in separate homes can work, like, if you're next door or in a duplex. If you really love your spouse, you won't get caught banging anyone's sister. And you can make things a little…spicy if you're creative enough," I say with a smile.

"All it takes is for one couple to accidently shoot each other to take that idea out of every married person's head," says Franklin with a snicker.

"You know, my grandmother was in a common law marriage, I think, until they made it official. They were together since I was a child and I never called him grandpa or anything like that. I called him Mister K. Even my grandmother would call him that sometimes. They were together for about 18 years before they made it official and stayed together for another 20 until he died. And they lived apart for at least…six months out of the year during a good portion of their marriage."

"You mean in separate houses?" asks Franklin.

"I mean in separate states. My grandmother had family property down south and Mister K. didn't like the South even though he was from Virginia. He stayed in New York and didn't go down unless he really had to. I guess in their case, that little piece of government paper didn't affect much."

"Oh, I don't know if I could go that far," he says as he uses a wide toothed comb through my fresh curls. "Why even get married if you can't live together? Separate bedrooms? Ok…maybe. Separate houses? Hmm…I dunno. But separate states? Naw, not me. If any female said to me let's get married and live in different states, I'd say no thank you."

"Long distance relationships aren't a new thing," I say. "Sometimes a person gets a job offer they can't refuse…and the couple work around the distance. Or they fell in love while living in different states."

"These young people can work around that distance with video chatting and whatnot, but they don't stay that way forever," says Franklin. "But older people, people my age, we don't use that technology like that. When we marry, we make plans to live in the same house in the same bed. You sharin' your life with a person, the good and the bad. It may not always be perfect, but that's how things are sometimes. I fell in love with my wife. I wanna see her face every day when I wake up in person, not through a phone or a laptop. When I have bad days, it's nice to know I have someone waitin' for me at home to hear all about it and take my mind off it. That's the good stuff about havin' someone permanent in your life. Because of that stuff, you put up with all the other stuff. It's a tradeoff."

"Hmm…," is the thoughtful sound I make as I mull over his words.

"What?"

"Well, it makes me wonder…if my grandmother and her husband ever really loved each other if they could live apart like that. As a matter of fact, that's how my marriage fell apart. My husband went away for military training temporarily and suddenly I didn't know him anymore. I even said to him before he left that I didn't think our marriage was strong enough for the separation and he said it had to be. Famous last words…that's what I thought when he said it.

Having experienced all of that, if I fell head over heels for someone, I'd want to be around him for the same reasons you mentioned, which are beautiful by the way. And even if I didn't like where we were living, I'd hope I could talk it over with my partner so we could do something about it."

Franklin gently lays his hand on my shoulder and says, "Exactly right" before he twirls the chair around so I can see my reflection in the mirror. For a moment I don't recognize the woman who has Franklin standing beside her, his arms folded on his chest, grinning with satisfaction.

"Who is that?" I ask as I turn my head to the left and the right, struggling to hold back tears.

"You like it?"

"I've…yes, I like it very much…I just… never thought I could wear my hair like this. It's—"

"Short and sassy, just like the person wearin' it," Franklin says, still grinning.

New Age Parenting

"I'm so sorry I'm late! Did you get my text message?" I say breathlessly as I quickly slide into a chair in the waiting area.

"You're good, relax," Franklin says as he finishes a customer.

I settle down and occupy my time with solitaire on my phone until he calls my name.

"So what happened?" he asks as he places the hairdresser cape around my neck.

"Well, I was at Ocean State Job Lot to pick up something real quick before coming here, but I got distracted in the parking lot."

"Distracted by what?"

I sigh and say, "There was this little boy, maybe about three years old, and he was in the parking lot…on the asphalt…throwing a tantrum. And the mother was gently talking to him to calm him down, but it just made things worse. She looked so stressed…and even though I should've minded my own business, I didn't."

"What'd you mean?" asks Franklin.

"I talked to the kid," I reply.

"And said what?"

"I got down to his eye level, which was basically the ground, and said, 'Young man, you stop this right now and get up! Your mother doesn't need this.'"

"And what happened?"

"He got up and stopped that crying, that's what. The mother thanked me…she really was stressed," I say, adding sarcastically, "And they walked off in peace…birds followed them into the store, the skies cleared…I think they skipped hand-in-hand from the parking lot."

"You a brave soul talkin' to someone's kid like that," says Franklin.

"I wouldn't say I was brave. If you saw what I saw, you'd try to help in some way. Plus, I wasn't disrespectful, I didn't yell at the child because he's not my kid. Kids need a firm voice sometimes and he responded to mine…they always do and I don't know why…even my own kids. I think they sense that I mean business, so don't try me! There's a time to yell and there's a time to use a firm voice. The first type you do at home…"

"And the second one you do in public!" finishes Franklin. "But you know what you did ain't always that simple. People don't want nobody tellin' them their business as a parent. That woman could've flipped out on you."

"Yeah, true. But I only break out the superpower when I feel it will be received. Listen, I was a single mom for a long time before I met my ex-husband and I *know* what it's like to feel…overwhelmed sometimes and wishing someone would step in when you're feeling…helpless I guess is the word for it. You don't know what to do, so you just stand there wishing whatever is happening will stop. The mother had that look…she was trying to negotiate with a toddler! You can't negotiate a toddler out of a tantrum. You have to take some type of action. When I was a kid, there was only one way to stop a tantrum in the middle of the street."

"An ass whoopin'!" chimes Franklin.

"Right! And people understood back then that an ass whoopin' was necessary and you didn't have to worry about being judged."

"And nine times outta ten it was just a swat or two on the backside…maybe shake 'em a little bit to let them know you meant business," he says with a chuckle as he runs his fingers through my hair.

"Threatening your kid through clenched teeth and saying, 'Wait 'til we get home!'. You knew you crossed the line then!"

"You do that today and people look at you like you're a criminal."

"But here's the hypocrisy in that…they *want* you to do something about it and deep down inside they *want* you to give that kid a swat or two, not negotiate or bribe that kid into silence. They don't want to stand in a long line at the supermarket hearing some kid scream their head off, and they don't want to admit that if they were at home with no one looking, they would do the swat. I hate to hear parents say, 'If you stop crying, I'll get you that toy you want.' If you gotta bribe your kid to behave, you got bigger problems than just a crying kid."

"Did the kid in the parking lot need a swat?" he asks.

"No! I've been a parent long enough to know when an action deserves a swat versus a firm voice. Toddlers are little people who can't express themselves when they're feeling funky. The trick is to know when they're doing something that's out of line or when they're just being fussy. And even if they're out of line, you still have to hold back a bit because you wanna teach them a lesson if you swat them, not scar them for life!"

"My little girl didn't act up like that at all," he says with a little pride in his voice. "She was quiet a lot of the time. We thought somethin' was wrong, but the doctor says that's just the way she is. She's still the same way…she has her little friends who are just like her. But they do say girls are different from boys. I got three boys and four girls. The girls stayed outta trouble mostly. The older ones had a school fight or two but nothing major. But the boys? They were a handful. Of course, it didn't help that I wasn't around to guide them. I don't have a lot of regrets in my life, but not being there for my kids is at the top of the list."

"I had two boys and for the most part they were good in public. If I said no to something they saw in the store, they understood no means no and they got on with it. Not a lot of tantrums at home either. But they did wreck my nerves on occasion.

One time they brought home a bucket of tadpoles they got from a creek behind our apartment complex, asking me if they could keep them. Another time, my younger one had this weird growth on his ankle. The doctor couldn't figure out what it was and recommended surgery. It looked like a wart to me, so I started putting hydrogen peroxide on it every day and dressing it. Within a week, that thing fell off. To this day I don't know what the hell that was!

One day I had to pick him up from daycare because he had a meltdown and had to be separated until I could get him. That happened a lot when he was little. He was about, maybe, four at the time. Luckily, I was only a ten-minute drive away, so I got him and brought him in to work until we had to close the office.

As we were leaving through the side door, my son broke loose and started running towards the street. I'm screaming at him to stop and before I know it, he's in the middle of the street and a car is coming. All I remember was the nose of a car and screeching tires."

Franklin stops his inspection of my hair and asks, "And then what happened?"

"My supervisor…her name was Carolyn, runs out in front of me into the street, snatches him up real quick, and brings him to the sidewalk. I was so petrified…I was literally frozen with fear."

"Whew! God was watchin' out for that child!"

"You know, my father had passed away not long before that happened. I'd like to think my father whispered to God to steer that car out of the way and give Carolyn, who was *over 60 years old*, the speed she needed to get my son. Did I spank him? Yell at him? Absolutely not! All I could do was hug him."

When Franklin is done inspecting my hair, he asks if I want a reshaping. For years I've always worn my hair short, mainly because stress and poor maintenance always prevented any significant length. But under Franklin's care, and by watching his technique, my hair was thriving. I ask him about the pros and cons of letting the style grow out and his answers make me decide to avoid a haircut this time and take a fresh color rinse instead.

"You ever heard of free-range parenting?" I ask Franklin as he's rinsing conditioner out of my hair.

"Free range? Naw, that's a new one on me. Free range…you mean like…let them go wherever they want?"

"Right."

"Without a parent around," he says.

"Yes."

"Ain't that what we did as children? Our parents kicked us out of the house? We did our homework…our chores… alright then, you can go and come back when the streetlights come on and not one minute later. You mean that?"

"That and walking to school by yourself, making decisions on your own—"

"Shoooot! When did all of that get the name free-range parentin'?" asks Franklin. "Why these young people gotta overthink stuff? It seems like they take somethin' old, put a new name on it, and claim they invented somethin' better. The way we were raised wasn't wrong—"

"Maybe a little misguided at times—"

"But not wrong! Yeah, ok, we got smacked around…maybe a little too much. And our parents were like…do as I say, not as I do. But some of the stupid stuff we did sometimes deserved a good smack! Especially if we were doin' something that would hurt us or somebody else. If we were disrespectful—"

"We got smacked," I say.

"If you laid hands on your parents—"

"You definitely got smacked," I say with a little laugh.

"It didn't guarantee you didn't do it again…maybe the laying hands was the one lesson that stuck. But not all lessons did…I'll admit to that."

"And you definitely knew the consequences if you did that thing again."

"But I tell you what, we were more self-sufficient!" exclaims Franklin. "And how many of us were…wadda call it…latchkey kids? You had that key around your neck that you couldn't lose or you'd get it bad! Came home by yourself, made a snack if you were hungry, and watched tv while you did your homework, then went outside to find your friends."

"I had a brother to take care of," I say in agreement.

"There you go! How's that for bein' able to make decisions on your own? Watchin' your little brother or sister, sometimes more than one. Man, get outta here with all that free-range nonsense!"

"Don't be shy, tell me how you really feel!"

"Free range parentin'," Franklin huffs before raising me from the sink. "Black folks been doin' free range parentin' from the moment they were kidnapped from Africa! Our ancestors were out in the fields pickin' cotton and whatnot as kids and was done when they heard the master's bell! No…child labor laws back then!"

"Speaking of that, there's another parenting style called 'lived consequences'."

As we walk back to his chair, Franklin asks, "What's that?"

"Well…it's like…not warning your kid before they step down a manhole."

"You lost me."

"Ok…say you have a set bedtime for your kid…9 p.m., right?" I say. "Your kid knows it's lights out at that time, but your kid wants to stay up longer. Instead of yelling at your kid to go to bed, you step away and say, ok, you want to stay up late? Alright, but I expect you up and ready for school on time the next morning, no excuses!"

"And what if the kid don't wake up on time?" he asks.

"Whatever happens the next morning is the consequence. If that means the kid wakes up late, doesn't get breakfast, misses the bus, falls asleep in class…all of those are the consequences."

"Ok, but ain't the parents gonna suffer those consequences as well?" asks Franklin. "Ain't that more work for the parent because they gotta fix the lateness by gettin' the kid to school if they missed the bus?"

"I think the hope is that the kid realizes how much of an inconvenience they caused by staying up late and won't do it again."

"What if there's a rule that they must clean their room every week? If the kid don't do it—"

"Then the consequences are a messy room that gets so bad you need a bulldozer," I reply.

"Hey, I ain't an expert when it comes to parentin'", says Franklin as he applies the color rinse to my hair with an applicator brush. "I'm still learnin'. But the one thing I do know is you can't just stand by and not do anythin' if your kid's in trouble or doin' somethin' wrong. Sometimes, you gotta warn them about that manhole, you gotta yell at them about cleanin' that damn room. Too many of us live in places where we got rats and roaches. And not all of us got medical coverage for our kid if they wind up in a…a… coma from fallin' down a hole. Our ancestors did everythin' possible to avoid consequences and made sure their kids knew too! It's about survival! Ain't no lettin' them step down a manhole when massuh is lookin' over your shoulder!"

"Agreed. If kids really did learn from their actions, why do we have so many juvenile detention centers with repeat offenders? It's more than just letting them learn consequences through their actions."

"If the kid messes up, and you told them it was gonna happen, it gives the parent…street cred with their kid, kinda," says Franklin. "You got a better chance of gettin' them to listen. That's why you need to provide that guidance!"

"I'll tell you…I still struggle with that," I say.

"With what?" he asks.

"Providing guidance. No, it's more like knowing when not to provide guidance when they got older.

I hate to throw race in the conversation, but there are certain things our kids, black kids, need to be aware of when they're out in the world. How to know when you're being treated differently because of your skin color, or how to fight back when you feel you've been wronged. Reminding them how to act when they get stopped by police. We have to teach them a different set of values and ways to behave because a certain group of people who judge and mislabel us think they're better than us. Some even view us as animals who need saving from ourselves. Our kids have to learn how to deal with that conflict in values and the nonsense that comes from all of that without becoming completely broken and perpetually frustrated. It's like you said, our ancestors screamed danger at their kids constantly because it was a matter of survival.

So, when my boys tell me about something that happened to them at their job, the momma bear in me is ready to tell them what to do to fix it! But I have to realize that they're adults and I can't always warn them…or protect them…or cuss out the bullies. There are some lessons that can only be learned by the consequences."

"It's about knowin' when to step back," says Franklin.

"It does. I started easing off the pedal when they turned 18. But when your kids are young, you need a balance between the free-range stuff and the authority stuff. Kids are only kids for a brief time in their lives when you think about it. Ten years…12 years…that's nothing in a life span that can last into your 80s, God willing. You have a window of opportunity to lay down some basic life lessons. You teach them to your kid over and over, hoping something will stick and stay by the time they're a teenager, and then an adult. You need to lay down the life lessons first and remind them…*repeatedly*… this is what happens when you do…this or that."

"And thump that head like a melon when they don't learn!" says Franklin.

Twisted Feminism

The summer is coming to an end, as well as a short-term contract I've been working, which means it's time to hustle with beast-like precision before the holidays approach and the job market slows down. The beast in me successfully yields two contracts that keep me too busy to schedule a hair appointment, which is ironic since I'm now flush with enough cash that could support bi-weekly appointments with Franklin if I wanted.

Though I've been doing a decent job at maintaining my hair, pushing my need for a relaxer or haircut to eight weeks instead of six, I'm ready to be spoiled. As I pick up my cell phone to call him, I hope he hasn't relocated his business again or even worse, stopped working altogether. But I need not worry; Franklin answers his phone, teases me briefly about my long absence and schedules my appointment at the same location when I last saw him.

I arrive on a busy Saturday morning and Franklin is unchanged and too cool for school as always. It is unseasonably but reasonably warm this October and Franklin is wearing his regular tank top with jeans attire, his bald, pecan tan head aglow and deeper in color.

"Hey stranger!" he greets me as I slide into his chair.

"Someone got a lot of sun this summer!"

"I took some time off with my family. My wife had been plannin' and payin' for this trip for us since last year."

"Where'd you go?"

"On a cruise to Bermuda. We left out of Miami. It was just for three days, but the whole trip was a week with the flights and hotel stays."

"I've never been on a cruise. I don't know if I could be trapped at sea for so long," I say.

"It really doesn't feel very long 'cause there's so much to do on the ship. You wanna eat? Gamble? Watch a show? Swim? The vacation ain't just the port call, although that was nice as well. Every day when they'd make the beds, they'd put…little animals made out of towels on my daughter's bed. She loved that."

"And what did *you* love about that trip?" I ask.

"I ain't sayin' 'cause it'll get me in trouble!"

"What do you mean by that?"

"If I say the thing I enjoyed the most, I'll get in trouble, so I'll keep my mouth shut."

"Now you have to tell me! You can't just drop that and expect me to ignore it. Say it…what did you enjoy the most?"

Franklin waits a moment as he examines my hair and then says, "The bikinis!"

"Oh Lord!"

"I ain't *never* seen so many styles of bikinis! Some look like one whole piece…barely anythin' being covered…just three small triangles of fabric connected by string coverin' certain areas if you catch my drift. Flesh was certainly exposed on that trip, all greased and tan with no hair anywhere! Hell, some of those bottom bikinis look like shrunken thongs. And the girls don't look old enough to be exposing so much flesh. I was strugglin' on that trip!"

"Struggling?"

"Not to look! And these young girls with all that flesh exposed were runnin' and jumpin' into water…good God! And I wasn't alone. I caught other dudes sneakin' looks at the same thing. Some didn't even try to hide it as they were standing next to their wives! Me? I was tryin' to be respectful 'cause I'm with my wife and child, but in my head I'm thinkin', 'God damn! Baby got cakes!'"

"Uh huh, do we need to discuss MeToo?" I ask as I shake my head in admonishment.

"I know all about MeToo. You can't live in a house with a paralegal and a little girl and not know about it! That's why I was strugglin' not to look."

"They don't make it easy for you men, huh?"

"They certainly do not! Us men, the straight men, we like female flesh, ok? In every shape, form and color! That's no secret. If you show us some female flesh, we gonna look at it! That's how we're built. Don't wear a bathing suit that shows us your money maker if you don't want us lookin' at you!"

"That's unfair and that's the point of the MeToo movement. Just because we're showing a little flesh, that doesn't mean you have to ogle us."

"That's settin' up us men for a whole lot of trouble and it ain't fair to us. Answer me this…why do women wear bikinis if they don't want men lookin' at them? Why are you at the beach? To swim or show off your body? You can get all the sun you need with just a regular bathing suit coverin' the good stuff. The ocean don't care about what you're wearin'. A good wave can come along and knock that piece of fabric off her body!"

"I can't speak for all women, but—"

"What kind of bathin' suit you wear?" Franklin persists.

"You can't go by me—"

"Why not? Just answer the question."

"I have what's called a tankini," is my reply.

"And what's that?"

"It's a two-piece bathing suit with a tank top and a skort for the bottom. A skort is like a mini skirt with shorts inside."

"Covers everythin' a man would appreciate a view of, don't it?"

I sigh before I reluctantly agree, "Yeah, it does."

"And why do you wear it?"

I sigh again before I respond, "Because right now my body isn't where it should be to wear a bikini."

"There you go! You don't want men lookin' at you, so you cover it up."

"That's not the only reason!" I argue. "I wear it because it's comfortable. When you're at the beach, there are places on a woman's body where sand shouldn't go. I don't want to spend the hour it takes to get to the beach diggin' sand out of my crack while I'm driving back. That's how I like it."

"Naw, you don't! Quit lyin'! If you felt you had the kind of body that went boom! pow! you'd be wearin' a bikini. And the only reason to wear one is to attract attention from *us men*!"

"Or other women if that's their thing."

"But women ain't complainin' about bein' sexually harassed by other women on the beach, are they?" he asks.

"I haven't heard anything, but you can't go by what I know. There are other places than the beach where such stuff can happen."

"But we ain't talkin' about other places. We're talkin' about the only place where you can see the most flesh! At a pool or a beach."

"Alright, I'll admit some women are dedicated to showing flesh in many places, at the beach, in the club, and so on. I don't have a problem with it…except at the supermarket."

"Why there?"

"Because why would you need to wear revealing clothing while you're shopping for pork chops and applesauce?"

"What if they're comin' home from work?" he teases me.

"What kind of job are you thinking of that requires a woman to dress that way?"

Franklin cackles before Nona, the owner of the shop who is listening in on our conversation, says, "I'm with you on that! Especially some of these young girls wearin'…spandex cat suits…showin' off their ass…at school! And those skinny tube dresses, bobbin' and weavin' on stripper heels? Lord have mercy! Let us pray!"

Those listening break out in laughter and when it dies down, I add, "It really is unreasonable to think men or young boys with hormones raging won't look."

"Thank you," he says before he renders judgment on my hair and the remedy: a relaxer, haircut and color rinse, nothing fancy this time.

As Franklin gets started, Ricki, the hairdresser next to Franklin's station, decides to chime in, "Wait, wait…hold up…there's nothing wrong with showin' off your body if you're proud of it. I got some outfits that show my shape and a little flesh. I like lookin' cute!"

"No, there's nothin' wrong with it," replies Nona. "But you can't show off your body and then complain men are lookin' at you. And makin' men feel bad for takin' a peek."

"Men take it too far sometimes, though," responds Ricki. "You got guys who keep it low key when they lookin', but then you get those men that are straight up dogs with it…like their whole vibe is about snatchin' up a side piece."

"Like the guys on the cruise. They didn't even hide they were lookin' with their wife nearby," says Franklin. "And grinnin' like a Cheshire cat at those girls, too. I ain't stupid enough to do somethin' like that."

"A guy parading around in a Speedo or a banana hammock with a cut body is doing the exact same thing…flaunting his body to attract attention," I say.

"But guys don't complain about bein' looked at! You don't see a movement about it, do you?" responds Franklin.

"That's because they jumped on the MeToo movement! They didn't have enough members to form their own club, so they jumped on the MeToo wagon! It wasn't just the victims of that movie executive that were writing op eds and giving interviews; there were a few men who spoke out too about being victimized, exploited..."

"I know the ones you're talkin' about…they were harassed by *other men*, not women," says Ricki.

"So what?" I say. "The imbalance of power still applies regardless of who is doing the harassing."

"But we're talkin' about what women go through and what men have been gettin' away with for years," says Ricki. "MeToo is about all those women who stayed quiet about bein' pressured into situations at work. Hey, I'm not sayin' a woman can't harass a guy. There's some crazy bitches out there, on the real!"

"I don't agree," says Nona.

"You don't agree with what?" responds Ricki.

"You said that MeToo was about women bein' pressured in work situations and kept it quiet, right?"

"Right."

"So, they were told by someone in charge that if you spread your legs for me, I'll do this for you…I'll give you that movie part you wanted, or a job with more money, but you need to keep your mouth shut."

"Probably somethin' like that," concedes Ricki.

"And if they said no, it meant the end of their career or whatever."

"Yeah, I guess."

"They kept quiet because they didn't want to lose what they were gettin'. If you got the truth on your side, what you afraid of? Honey, if they call you a liar, you fight them! If you lose that job, good riddance!

Or they could've avoided all of that by sayin', 'I ain't doin' that!' and whatever happens, happens. Us regular people start over every damn day…we get fired from a job, we find another one or switch into a new profession. That's what I did! I was workin' in insurance and got fired and I decided to start my own business. So, why couldn't they do that?"

"Amen!" shouts a chorus of other hairdressers.

"I heard stories about women invited to meetings in hotel rooms and I'm like…what? Huh?" continues Nona. "I don't know about you, heifers, but I know my momma didn't teach me to go a man's hotel room *by myself*! She was always warnin' me about these men and what they be up to. No self-respecting young lady, if she's raised right, goes to a man's room like that, simple as that. If a man is askin' you to his hotel room, he's only got one thing on his mind. Ain't that right, Franklin?"

"I plead the Fifth!" quips Franklin. Snickering from those listening immediately follows his comment.

"My momma would say goin' to a room of a man you don't know ain't proper," says Nona. "If you need privacy to talk your business, that's what an office is for."

"See? That's what I'm talkin' about," says Ricki. "Women were gettin' harassed there too! They were preyed upon no matter where they were."

"Ok, they were gettin' harassed everywhere. Why didn't they quit that job? Tell that man to back off? What's more important? Your soul and self-respect or your bank account?"

Again, the chorus of those listening shout amen, followed by a few slow claps.

"Hold on," I say. "Sometimes it's not as simple as quitting a job. MeToo talks about the workplace, sure, but it's not just there.

A couple of years ago I had a small lump on my scalp in the back…had it for years and finally decided to get rid of it, which meant surgery. So, I make an appointment and I'm assigned a doctor…I call him Dr. Feel Good.

At the consultation, I'm sitting in one of the extra chairs in the room as he walks in. He looks at me, asks me some questions about why I'm there, and then he asks me to stand so I can show him where the lump is."

"Wait, hold up," says Nona holding up a hand. "Not sit on the exam table? Why the hell do you need to stand for him to see somethin' on your scalp? It was on your scalp, right? Like…back here?" She points to the area and I nod.

"Baby girl, you don't need to stand up for somethin' like that! You could've bowed your head in the chair you were sittin' in!"

"You know, that day I was so nervous because other than a C-section I've never had surgery…no broken bones, knock on wood. I do everything I can to stay out of a doctor's office. I didn't know what to expect and I had no reason not to trust the person who's gonna cut my scalp open! He said he needed me to stand so he could see it better.

Instead of me standing up on my own, he comes over and holds his hand out to pull me up…like guys used to do when pulling a girl up to dance. He asks me more questions as he somehow maneuvers me to stand with my back to him and I reach up to part my hair so he can see it."

"Hold up," interrupts Ricki as she pushes off the chair she's been leaning on. She imitates what I've just described, which is basically the stance one would be in if being frisked by the police and I nod in agreement when she looks over her shoulder.

"Guuurlll!" exclaims Ricki as she turns back around.

"Seeing it now as you've done it…I feel stupid for not questioning it," I say, "but he threw me off guard because he was so quiet after I did what he asked…he didn't say anything for a while and the silence just…messed with my head…none of what's happening is making sense to me, but we're trained to defer to a man in a white coat, aren't we?

Then he suddenly starts talking after I've been standing in that position for a good…I dunno…15? 20 seconds? Try sitting for 15 seconds in silence and see how long it can be, especially when you're anticipating a next step. Because my back is to him, I don't know how close he is to me or what he's doing behind me, so when he suddenly starts talking…I was a little shook. He says he'll have to put me under anesthesia and then disappears for 20 minutes to look for a consent form. Even the nurse came in after a while asking where he was. I left that office so confused and feeling all of that shit was weird."

"That was weird," agrees Franklin. "I got no explanation for that."

"So, as the surgery gets closer, something tells me to take a local anesthetic instead of going under. The cyst wasn't that big, the side of a pea, so I felt it would be better to strength a lidocaine needle and numb the spot."

"Yes, girl," says Nona. "Anesthesia ain't nothin' to play with. You don't know what is goin' on while you're under."

"Exactly. When they call to give me pre-op instructions, I tell the nurse I want a local and she said I can make that known before I go into surgery, but she'll make a note in my chart. Ok, cool.

The day of the surgery, Dr. Feel Good is walking around the floor in a wool coat with scrubs underneath, looking all kinds of anxious as I'm waiting. He finally comes in, says he heard my request for a local, and says that's fine. I get in the operating room and it's a resident who cuts out the cyst while Dr. Feel Good is standing nearby. And because it's in the back of my head, I have to lay on the operating table face down, ass up, propped by a pillow under my hips to ease my back.

They sew me up and Dr. Feel Good says *the resident* will visit me in the recovery ward, *the resident* will give me post op instructions. Guess who shows up just as I'm getting dressed?"

"Dr. Feel Good," guesses Nona, arms folded across her chest.

"Yup! I tell him to hold on as I finish, then he comes in. Now, the ward was practically empty; there was one other person opposite me. Because of that, the lights were in energy saving mode…it was dim but not completely dark. There we are, just he and I standing with a bed nearby and his pupils, he had blue eyes, are dilated like crazy because the lights are low, making the situation even creepier."

"Oh, he was white?!" exclaims Nona.

"*Of course* he was white!" is my reply. "Black surgeon? Never have I ever seen one up here!"

"What's that bit with Chris Rock?" says Franklin. "About seein' Native Americans? You ain't never see two Native Americans together at the same time! One month you might see one, maybe three months later you might see another one."

"When it comes to black surgeons, try three years later!" quips Nona.

"Wait, hold up, ya'll," says Ricki. "Ya'll missin' the point of what she just said. That guy could've done anything to her!" Then she turns to me and asks, "Weren't you scared?"

I think about her question for a moment before I respond, "I know this sounds odd, but I wasn't too concerned. Think of what he's risking by making a false move at his place of work. Like I said, there was someone recovering across the aisle and if I screamed or anything, a whole lot of people would come running. I just kept my distance, and he kept his as he gave me the instructions.

To me he's, like…prolonging it. I'm not an idiot…I understand the concept of not washing my hair for two weeks to avoid reopening the incision. Business concluded…he leaves then I leave to meet my older son who's in the waiting area because he drove me there just in case I was put under. Just as we're approaching the parking garage, guess who comes out at the same time?"

"Are you kiddin' me?" asks Ricki. "Oh, that ain't coincidence."

"That's what I thought at the time, too. I'm glad my son was with me that day. Now, get this…we're chatting and on that day it was cold and rainy, sleet on the ground. Again, he's going over the instructions and says, 'Don't forget to keep it wet!' and I say, 'You mean don't forget to keep it dry, don't you?'"

Franklin and those listening burst out laughing.

"'Yeah, yeah, keep it dry,' he says and he disappears," I say.

Another round of laughter follows before I continue my story:

"Three weeks later I visit him for the follow-up. That morning I had to get my younger son to court and he wanted to get there early, around 9 a.m. or so. My appointment was at 8 a.m. and I deliberately got there 10 minutes early so he can see me on time because it takes 20 minutes to get back home.

He finally shows up in the exam room 20 minutes after eight, wearing a suit with a mis-matched tie. He greets me and I'm a little pissed off by this time. We have some small chit chat, then he asks me to stand. We're staring at each other as I'm waiting for him to tell me what to do next. All of a sudden, he comes in close and pulls me into a *hug*!"

"He did what?!" says Ricki, Franklin and Nona simultaneously.

"He hugs me! Bear hug! I'm looking at the ceiling, just hella confused and feeling like I should hug back. Then he pulls away and says, 'You look like you needed a hug'."

"What in the *hell?*" exclaims Nona. "How old was this doctor?"

"I dunno…young but not too young, like late 30s, early 40s."

"Sounds like Dr. Feel Good needed to feel somethin' good!" jokes Franklin.

"That's why I call him that. He *jedi mind tricked me* into a hug as Eddie Murphy would say! I'm standing there after he did it, thinking, 'Ok, maybe I really did need a hug.'"

"He forced you into a hug, girl!" exclaims Ricki. "Violated your personal space and then on top of that, have you standin' there like a slave on the auction block bein' sized up! You can't report that! What you gonna say if you complain? He hugged me? He made me stand like I was being frisked? See? That's exactly what I'm talkin' about. That right there is some sick ass, MeToo behavior!"

Excited by my story, the animated conversation continues as Franklin leads me to the sinks to wash out the relaxer cream.

"See what you started?" says Franklin, grinning, as he washes my hair. "I gotta watch my back today!"

Religion Needs Faith

It is quiet today. It feels as though New England has stopped in mid movement and all you can hear is the ticking of a stopwatch. However, it's the inhabitants of the Nutmeg state who are fruitlessly attempting to process the chaos and confusion. Though the continuance of life is reflected in the traffic, in the stores and on the streets, there is a funeral flow to the hustle and bustle. Grief has enveloped the state and as more details are broadcasted over every major and non-major news network, drawing in more people who share the information with others, the sadness grows heavier. The "telephone, telegraph, tell a friend" method to spread news has been replaced by "tweet, post, share." All social media feeds are now flooded with details big and small.

Unfortunately for nutmeggers, especially those living in the Western part of the state, December 14, 2012 was their 9/11, their JFK assassination. People living in the surrounding area can probably remember where they were when the news of Sandy Hook was first made known and the town was practically on lock down. As the body count grew, grief mixed with horror, anger and frustration began to mount. It did not matter whether those who fell into the eternal were known intimately. We wanted accountability. We wanted answers. Immediately.

On this day, I am conflicted as well as in disbelief. Today is my hair appointment with Franklin, which was scheduled a week prior. I text Franklin to confirm our appointment and he signals back that I can come. While in my car to the salon, I tune into the radio for updates and when I hear the names and ages of those no longer with us, especially the ages of the little ones, I bow my head and take a moment before entering the salon.

As I walk in, CNN is on the wall-mounted TV and everyone is watching intently as they shake their heads or cover their mouths in shock. The beauticians try to work while watching the news, talking in hushed tones with their client in the chair.

"How you doin'?" Franklin says somberly as I slip into his chair.

"I'm not sure," I respond as he drapes the hairdresser's cape around me. "This is the first time in my life that I wanted to news to be false. Especially this type of news. I keep thinking about all those babies—"

"That could've been my daughter," he says in a low-key voice. "The one place you thought your kids would be safe was school and look what happens. It don't make sense to me."

"It doesn't make sense to anybody with a heart and soul, really. Your heart would have to be coal black to not feel something."

"Like the piece of shit who shot 'em," he says angrily. "Pardon my language."

"That's the first time I've heard you cuss."

"This is the first time you've seen me angry, that's why."

"You know, I've always been on the fence about whether God exists. But as a child, I was trained to believe, so it's been hard for me to turn my back on all of that. But after today…I dunno…"

"You mean if there is a God, how could He let that happen," he says, his voice monotone.

"That or anything else in this world where innocent people die needlessly at the hands of another. It feels like a blood clot is forming and the pressure in the veins is building and just about to blow. It scares me that there is such…evil in people's hearts. Everybody is jumping on the mental illness bandwagon, and I'm thinking where is the responsibility? Do we just ignore the evil with the excuse the shooter wasn't in the right frame of mind?"

"Hey, I haven't been to church in a while. But I do believe in God; I believe that Jesus died for our sins irregardless of proof or whatever people need to believe in his sacrifice. I've had many low moments in my life, and I came through all of 'em 'cause God looked out for me and brought people into my life to help me. Without God, I don't know where I would be."

"So how do you convince non-believers that God exists after today?"

"Are you a non-believer now?" Franklin counters.

I pause for a moment, trying to contain my tears as the TV shows a Brady Bunch-style gallery of photos with names and ages of the little ones. I swallow the lump in my throat and croak out my weak response:

"I don't know."

I feel Franklin's slender hands rest gently on my shoulders from behind and squeeze lightly.

"God is not responsible for what happened today," he says in a firm, gentle voice. "An asshole in a home with no values or respect for human life is responsible. And I'll take it one step further…if a black person had all those weapons, how long do you think the police would let them keep 'em? Do you think they'd see that black person as a gun collector or up to no good even if they purchased them legally? You see how many guns the mother and son had between 'em? Thousands of dollar's worth! What you need anti-assault guns for? What invasion you expectin' in this state? Naw, God ain't responsible for that. Don't put that on God. Laws that shield people who own a ridiculous amount of guns are responsible."

"Is this about to be a discussion on gun control?"

"Not today it ain't! I'm tired of that same 'ole discussion of the Second Amendment or other such nonsense! And I ain't got much to say on it other than fix the laws to control how much guns people buy," he says.

"People do go around and around on the subject," I agree.

"And the fix is so easy! That's the messed up part. They ask the same questions, do the same talkin' and still nothin' is done. Man, forget all that! Stop playin' around and do what needs to be done!"

"Laws and policies aren't on people's radar when you see children cut down like that. Believers probably see God as a being who has to power to stop mass murder, who can control the evil in the world. I'm not the only one who expects God to step up and stop this kind of ruin."

"That's one mistake right there. God don't work that way."

"What are you talking about?! The Bible outlines in Genesis that He *does* work that way! He flooded the lands, made Noah build that ark! He swept the lands clean of evil people!"

"Don't you think that some of those people might have been children? It's possible, ain't it?" argues Franklin.

"Yeah, it's possible. But we're talking about sweeping away evil. Children aren't evil."

"If they ain't being raised right, they can be."

"But they could also be innocent. There's no way to know for certain whether God foresaw their future and decided to sweep the land. For non-believers and people on the fence like me, that's a hard sell if you're trying to bring us over to the believers' side. All we see are children and adults dying way too soon, a good portion of them cut down before they were even able to decide on a path of good or evil. For me, I think like a child, and I say that's not fair, it's not right, and if that's the way God operates, then no thank you, I can do without religion."

"No one who's a believer understands God's ways," says Franklin. "And we weren't meant to understand 'em. People think God can solve everything, but that's not what He's here for."

"Then what is He here for?" I ask.

Franklin is quiet for a moment as he combs through my hair. He stops and says,

"To make sure everythin' runs as it should be."

"So, God has a plan?"

"No, I don't think that," says Franklin. "God don't plan; He just…does."

"That's why religion has no faith. People don't like the things He does and they find it difficult to have faith in another human being's interpretation of gospel when mass murder happens around them. And it doesn't have to be the crazy shooter kind of mass killing; you see it in wars and genocides, in government overthrows, in massive drug overdoses and gang shootouts. And when people like me question that, you hear the cliché response: it's part of God's plan."

"I don't say that."

"No, you don't," I say gently. "I wish more believers said it as you do. I can process the thought of God making sure things run as they should rather than it being His plan because it brings up the question of why God would plan for children to die?"

"It turns God into someone who's bad and wants bad things to happen."

"It turns God into a person," I say.

"It does," agrees Franklin.

"And God is not a person with feelings or is ruled by emotions."

"Naw, God ain't like that."

"Then we should stop referring to God as a He. Using that pronoun implies a lot, don't it? There are expectations when you refer to God as He or She."

As Franklin grabs his clipper to clean up the hair at the nape of my neck, he says, "I never thought about it."

"Because that wasn't something you questioned growing up. I never questioned it. I was taught God is He, the almighty father and Jesus was His son. And He and His are capitalized to show due reverence."

"Sounds familiar."

"But God isn't Morgan Freeman! When we use human pronouns for an infinite being, you automatically give God human characteristics, which can then set us up for disappointment because we expect God to respond as a human would. A decent human would stop that atrocity. A human can take immediate, tangible action.

I think we extend our reverence for God onto priests and pastors and reverends. We expect the people who uphold scripture to be free from selfish ways, to be free from corruption, to be holy and perfect. And when they aren't these things, we question why we should go to church. Why should I believe these people in cleric robes who tell me to be good if I want a blessed life and afterlife?"

"Ain't religion about faith as you said?" asks Franklin. "The people who still go to church every week have faith that whatever they're learnin' will help 'em. That whoever is teaching them is a God-fearing person."

"But those numbers are decreasing. People don't go to church like they used to. Christianity and Catholicism aren't the ruling forces they used to be. And I find that people don't have respect for religion anymore. This scares me too because religion contains morals that establish our code of conduct, really. It outlines how we should treat each other. Our laws are based around those moral principles, and this is why murdering a person can put someone in the gas chamber as a punishment…the 'eye for an eye' thing."

"Hammurabi's code," says Franklin.

"Oh, you know about the code, huh?"

"My grandpa made sure I knew about that code. Grandpa knew his Bible back to front, could recite chapter and verse. He knew the Old Testament and always said it followed that code. The book of Deuteronomy was his favorite because the slaves are free and about to enter the Promised Land. He would school me on how Canada and Nova Scotia were the promised land for black slaves here."

"This side of you is interesting, Franklin."

"I aim to please!"

"But if you ask half of these young folks what Hammurabi's code is, they couldn't tell you."

"People got a short memory when it's convenient," says Franklin. "Learnin' about the Bible and the code was more acceptable when I was growin' up. Kids could have a children's Bible without it becomin' a thing to be argued about."

"I remember looking forward to the Advent calendars at Christmas. Remember those?"

"Yeah, with the little chocolates inside, with a quote from scripture under each flap," says Franklin, nodding in agreement.

"When I was a kid, you dressed your Sunday best," I say. "Shirt and tie for the boys; cute dresses and itchy tights for the girls. The women with their big, colorful hats with dresses to match; the men in suits or a clean shirt and tie. Yeah, you were uncomfortable for a couple of hours; girdles were fit to burst, and the perfume faded earlier than you had hoped. But you went through the trouble to show respect for the church and by extension, God. Now, they show up in jeans and sneakers…street clothes. Regardless of how I feel about church, you should…you know… show respect for the institution."

"Lemme ask you a question," says Franklin.

"Shoot."

"When Jesus had his traveling ministry, do you think the followers wore colorful hats and pressed suits? What you think they wore? Go on and say it! You know the answer!"

"Linen or sackcloth…tunics, robes, I guess," I concede reluctantly.

"Ok then…does it really matter what people wear to church today? So long as people are presentable with whatever they got for clothes, they're welcome in church. That's how these ministers think today. Why force people to dress up if they ain't got the money to do it?"

"Are you suggesting I'm old fashioned in my thinking?" I tease him.

"Don't put words in my mouth!" exclaims Franklin. "All's I'm sayin' is…churches can't be picky about how people dress when they tryin' to minister to drug dealers and prostitutes, gettin' them in church. You expect those people to have respectable suits and dresses? Are you sayin' they shouldn't be allowed in church because they ain't got a decent dress?"

"No, I'm not saying that."

"Alright then!" gloats Franklin.

"But setting aside dress codes, today, people seem to turn to religion when it suits them and then turn away when they've got what they needed. Like people in prison. They violate the law, go to prison, and then find religion. If they indeed have found God, why do some wind up back in prison? Do you know the two top things inmates discuss in prison? It's how to beat their case, or how they found God and got saved."

"That's what religion is for!" he exclaims, playfully tapping me on my shoulders. "Religion is for people who have no one to turn to, who don't have strong values. They have no one to listen to 'em! If you're in trouble and can't talk to a person, you can talk to God. It don't matter when or where they pick up religion, just so long as they pick it up!"

"Yes, it does! If they picked up religion before they violated the law, do you think they'd be in jail?"

Franklin considers my question before responding, "Probably not. But it depends on if they understand and follow the word. You can go to church every Sunday and swear by God, but if you don't embrace the word, all of it don't mean a damn thing."

"No argument here," I say. "If you have no fear of damnation for the sins you commit, going to church won't help you. Let's be honest, our faith hinges on fear of what might happen if we don't follow the Bible. Those who believe don't want their soul to reside in everlasting torment."

"I know I don't want that! I do what I can to stay away from the flames!"

"You know what surprises me? The Catholics are losing numbers. *The Catholics!*"

"That ain't no surprise with all them priests doin' stuff with children," says Franklin. "Me followin' the word of God with a bunch of pedophiles tellin' me *I'm* a sinner? Naw, not me!"

"I think the new generation expects a lot from church and if they don't get it, they use it as an excuse for not going."

Franklin stops cutting and says, "You know, that's true. Did I tell you one of my daughters is gay?"

"Of course not! Where are you going with this?"

"Well, I agree with you because my daughter says she won't attend a church that don't support…LQB…"

"LGBTQ+ rights," I correct him.

"Yeah, she said if a church don't embrace her choice of lovin' a woman, she won't go to church."

"But does she practice a religion? Did she go to a different church?"

"Hmmm…I don't know. I never thought to ask her."

"So, your daughter is saying if they don't want me in their church, I ain't going! But you don't hear them say what they're doing to replace that."

"Wadda you mean replace it?" Franklin asks as he resumes cutting my hair.

"How do they worship? If you think church is intolerant and corrupt, what do you do to strengthen your relationship with God? I didn't raise my sons in the church, but my older son is a born-again Baptist. When he was in his early 20s, he started getting curious about religion, so I gave him books I had on Catholicism, Islam, Buddhism, Hinduism…even Daoism so he could see how they work. Anything about Christianity I answered, and he had a friend who was Jewish who'd answer any questions he had about Judaism. I had no idea he made a choice and got baptized until he told me much later and I was like, how did I *not* notice my son coming home soaking wet on a Sunday?"

"You don't think they walk around church in wet clothes after they take the dip, do you?"

"I saw one once," I say.

"Saw one what?" asks Franklin.

"A baptism, an adult one, during the rare occasion when I attended church because my son asked me to. The baptism pool, you could step down into it, was above the pulpit, like, in a room with glass as a wall so the entire congregation could watch."

"Like at Sea World."

"Yeah, a human version of Sea World but less splashy and more holy," I say as Franklin tilts my head to the side to cut around my ear. "The lights in the church were dimmed and the pool area was the only thing lighting the church. You could see the people enter the pool area wearing the baptism robe and the pastor was down below on a mic guiding the baptism that was broadcasted through a speaker in the room. It was…entertaining and moving at the same time, you know? Guess what I was praying for?"

"What?"

"That the glass didn't shatter or the floor of that room didn't cave in below, like a real version of Genesis when all that water comes rushing out. Not how uplifting the ceremony was, just potential disaster. And I was thinking, 'How do you insure a pool like that?' and 'How do the black women protect their hair because I know that pool must be chlorinated. Are they allowed to wear a swim cap?'"

"That's what you got out of that?!" exclaims Franklin.

"Well, no… I mean…I can see how cleansing that baptism could be for a person. But you can't help but be curious about stuff like that when you see such a spectacle. How many times in your life have you seen a baptism pool over a church pulpit?"

"Never! But I know I wouldn't be thinkin' about wet hairdos and pool insurance!"

"Anyway, getting back to the subject, my son takes on responsibilities at the church and one of them is bus captain for the buses that transport parishioners who live far away. He told me the story of twin girls, 14 years old, and both of them have girlfriends."

"Girlfriends? You mean as in friends who are girls? Or as in dating?"

"Dating. Apparently, the twins were…are lesbians. I mean, I assume they still are. These young people switch off tracks like speeding trains, like they invented bisexuality."

"Fourteen-year-old lesbian twins with girlfriends, huh?" says Franklin. "I gotta tell my wife about this one. Alright then. Go on."

"So, one of them asks my son if the church supports LGBTQ rights."

"Well, do they?"

"According to my son, he didn't feel comfortable speaking on behalf of the church like that, so he said he wasn't sure and told her to talk to the pastor. The twin responds that if the church doesn't support those rights, she and her sister would stop coming. And they did."

"Stop comin'?" asks Franklin.

"Yep."

"Because the church doesn't welcome them?"

"I dunno. They didn't show up the following Sunday. My son didn't know if they talked to the pastor or not. Kinda unfair to ghost the church if they didn't talk about it," I say, shrugging my shoulders.

"They were using that as an excuse to get out of going to church probably."

"My question is why do you need a brick-and-mortar church to worship and pray? Jesus didn't teach in a building."

"No, he did not!" agrees Franklin. "His ministry was everywhere. Jesus and his apostles taught in gardens, by riversides, and on the road."

"Exactly! And if you believe in the existence of a god, then you have to believe that God is everywhere because of the omnipresence that an infinite being possesses, right? God is not just in a church; God is everywhere and just like you said earlier, you can talk to God at any time. Putting conditions on a church and stomping your foot when that church doesn't accept your ways is confusing as hell to me. Find another church if you must."

"You know what I'd look for in a church if I started goin' back?" asks Franklin.

"No. What?"

"I'd wanna know what is the church doin' for the community? What are they doin' with the money I tithe? That, for me, would be the best way to show that they doin' right by God's word, providin' service for those who don't have a lot. If I see a pastor drivin' around in a Mercedes and the church hasn't expanded or done stuff for the neighborhood, you can bet I ain't attendin' that church 'cause I know some of my dollars went to that Mercedes."

"Better still, go to your backyard if you have one or go to a park, sit under a tree, and *talk to God!*" I say. "Aren't we always told the power is within us? Do your prayer. Say what's bothering you. Pray for strength and guidance if that's what you need, but don't *demand* things from a church that you can easily provide to yourself."

"Prayer is about easin' sufferin'," Franklin says absently as he tilts my head to the other side to continue cutting.

"To unburden your heart. I know that the Bible is problematic. It's filled with old language and customs that don't apply anymore and stories that are difficult to swallow. Was it possible for Sarah to give birth to Isaac at 91 years old back then? Did Moses really part the Red Sea?"

"Without messin' around with nature? Nope!"

"But we have *faith* that it happened. Faith is about believing in something blindly even though there's uncertainty. And I think people have lost that ability to believe blindly. If a church wants more followers, then the clergy has to stop pretending they're holier than thou and start admitting that they are just as human as their followers and not above sin—"

"And admit to their shortcomings," adds Franklin.

"Yes! Admit to them! We may all be made in God's image, but we are flawed. And if people understood that church may not have all the answers, but you can at least find some relief from whatever turmoil you're in and find community, then they wouldn't be so dissatisfied because they didn't see quick results."

"I don't think you lost your faith like you say you do," he says. "You say you might be a nonbeliever, but at the same time you wonder where was God and why didn't He protect those children? Why bring God into the conversation if you don't have faith that He exists?"

A small sigh escapes my lips before I reply, "When I would spend the night at my grandmother's house as a child, she would make me say the Lord's prayer at bedtime, which she taught me, every night I was there. Not the short version, the long version."

"From Sermon on the Mount," he adds. "The Matthew version."

"That's the one, along with the praise response:

> *For thine is the kingdom*
> *And the power*
> *And the glory*
> *Forever and ever*
> *Amen*

She taught me that prayer when I was…seven, maybe? Forty-something years later and I still remember it. I think she taught it to me so I wouldn't fumble over the words at her funeral."

"She passed on?" he asks quietly.

"Yeah, in body, but not in spirit. She's still around in her own way."

"You believe that?"

"Only because I was trained to think that way. My mother's side was a mix of religion and the metaphysical, where past relatives visit you in your sleep."

"Wait a second," counters Franklin. "You a grown woman. Isn't that what you women say? You a grown woman with your own mind. You may have been raised that way, but you still hold on to that way of thinkin' because deep in your heart, you still believe. And that need to believe ain't got nothin' to do with how you were raised."

"I only have one thing to say to that."

"What?"

I turn around to meet his gaze and say, "There but for the grace of God, go I."

No Justice, No Peace

Four Christmases have passed since Sandy Hook gripped my state in sorrow. Once the timeline of events was established and the details fleshed out, it only ingrained the sadness deeper. Legislation was enacted, going so far as to prevent Freedom of Information requests for investigation information, but it still doesn't seem to be enough to make people feel as though everything that can be done has been done. Investigations found more questions than answers, but it doesn't prevent the discussion of mental health and a cognitive disability as a cause. The school is torn down and rebuilt, and the house of the shooter's family, which no person in their right mind would buy, is bought by the town and demolished. Conspiracy theorists flock to social media to preach their gospel. Lawsuits are filed and settlements out of court allow the parents to move on somewhat, yet you can hear the pain from them in interviews. Nothing seemed to change significantly, same waltz, different tune. School shootings continue across the country in middle and high schools and universities, with varying numbers of loss of life.

The new year brings me a permanent job. I have been growing weary of the hustle needed to pursue contracting work. I prove to be the product of the baby boomer generation, believing a job with benefits is the more secure route to take in adulthood, especially when you're still supporting children, albeit near adult ones.

The job is an hour's drive one-way, which means getting up before the butt crack of dawn. This makes for long days and being robbed of precious sleep time, making me cranky and stressed. The job doesn't pay well, so I find a side hustle that unfortunately taxes my energy even further. The adjustment to a new job, taking on more work and other life changes make my visits to Franklin a must-have, for it is my only time to be pampered and take a break from life.

"Your hair is gettin' thin in some areas," says Franklin after he examines my hair during one such visit. "And it's breakin' off a lot. Your hair feels dry."

I sigh and say, "I've noticed that, too. I was hoping you wouldn't notice."

"You can't hide hair problems from me. Many have tried and failed. Have you been deep conditionin' your hair?"

"When I remember to. I've got so much going on right now—"

"Oh, are you keepin' busy again?" jokes Franklin.

Before I can answer, my cell phone rings and, after viewing the number, I quickly excuse myself to take the call outside of the salon. When I return to Franklin's chair, he asks as he drapes a black cape around my neck,

"Everything ok?"

"Yeah, yeah," I say quietly. "That was my son. I try not to miss his calls…he doesn't always get access to the phones."

"Wait," Franklin says, stopping his inspection of my hair. "This your older son or the younger one?"

"The younger one."

"I thought he lived with you."

"He does," I confirm. "But right now, he doesn't."

"He moved out?"

"Not exactly. Not if you call going to jail moving out."

Franklin pauses his actions and says, "Oh! so that's what you meant by access to the phones."

Afraid to burst out in tears in front of chatting strangers, I merely nod.

"Damn!" swears Franklin. "I hate to hear another story about another brothah gettin' caught in the system. How long he got?"

"This time nine months."

"What you mean 'this time'? What he do?" he asks.

"Violate probation. This is the second time. The last time he got six months."

"And how long this been goin' on where he gets violated and then put back on probation?"

"Four years thereabout," I answer.

"And how long was his original sentences supposed to be for?"

"Three years."

"Say what?" responds Franklin, incredulous. "He coulda served straight time instead of messin' around with probation! Where's he servin' his time?"

I lower my voice and respond, "Cheshire."

"Cheshire!" whispers harshly. "What the hell did he do to wind up there?"

"That's part of the problem. He's not supposed to be there. He's under 20, so he's supposed to be at the youth facility across the street from Cheshire. But because of his charge, even though he's considered a youthful offender when it happened, they put him in Cheshire. I haven't slept right since he's been there."

"Damn!" exclaims Franklin. "I'm really sorry. I know a few folks that served time there and that place ain't no joke! One dude I know was servin' time when those two guys escaped and did that thing to that family."

"I think about that every time I go to visit him," I say, shaking my head with worry. "Cheshire is, like, 40 minutes away, plopped right in the middle of a residential area. I'm lucky; I have a car. But I think about all those families who don't have access to a car and have to rely on other people to visit or try to get a shuttle if one is offered because there's no public transportation that goes directly there. When I drive up, I feel like I'm in the movie The Shawshank Redemption. Every time I visit him, I immediately want to turn around and go home. I can't stand it. It takes everything in me to get out of my car."

Franklin, sensing my voice is about to crack, offers me a tissue and I thank him before wiping my eyes. We stay silent for a moment as I compose myself. Franklin then offers his waste basket for my used tissue and hands me a fresh one.

"Thank you," I whisper, taking a deep breath.

"How's he doin' in there?"

I shake my head before responding, "Not very well. He finally got some meds to help for the anxiety, but he's afraid to take them because they put him in such a deep sleep that he snores. His cellmate…excuse me, his 'cellie' complained and he's trying not to piss off his cellie."

"Yeah, you ain't always gonna get a cell to yourself and even if you do, you won't have it that way for very long. You can't make enemies in prison; it ain't healthy, especially with your cellie. It don't make for a good livin' situation."

"He tells me stories, but I have a feeling he doesn't tell me everything and I don't think I want to know it all."

"Hey, you don't need to know everythin', little mama," he says firmly. "Trust me on that. All you need to do is go up there and make sure his head is right and keep his spirits up. Those visits can mean a lot to a brothah that's been locked in a tiny cell with some dude he don't know…could be a killer for all you know."

"Is this what you call making someone feel better?"

"I'm sorry, I'm sorry. I'm just tryin' to keep it real for you."

"Too real. I just…I hate going up there. I have to make sure I've got quarters for the lockers to lock up my keys and stuff. I think it's so sad that I know the routine by heart now…I avoid wearing jewelry and anything metal so I can quickly go through the metal detector. I sit with mothers and wives and girlfriends and grandmothers…kids and babies…and wait until they call you."

"And the kids really don't understand why they can't hug their daddy," says Franklin. "And they won't forget how they saw their daddy in jail."

"It's better for the babies than the older kids. As a parent, I feel for the mothers who have to explain their daddy is serving time and you won't see him for a while."

"Think about the grandmas who gotta take on those kids when the mother goes to prison," says Franklin. "And it's always the grandmas...no grandpas."

"Especially when you have to deal with social services and protective services, who are always understaffed and bureaucratic. When you genuinely ask for help, you get the runaround. You wind up jumping through more flaming hoops than a circus poodle for most of these agencies. But they won't hesitate to jump in your business and accuse you of this or that, often based on a lie. There are rachet people who use protective services like a weapon against someone they don't like."

"To jam you up! Amen to that!" Franklin sings back.

"You know what I hate the most when I visit? I have to sit on a cold metal stool and wait to see my son walk to a booth behind plexiglass and pick up some dirty phone, wearing God awful...beige prison shit! I can't hug him, I can't hold his hand...all I can do is tell him about the latest Boondocks episode and offer small chit chat."

"You do what now?" Franklin asks with a little chuckle.

"You know the animated series The Boondocks? My sons like watching it. I started watching recently because that series has a lot to say. The new season came out, so I've been filling him in after each episode…trying to make him laugh, making the best use of the hour I get to see him."

"Hey, if it works, then keep doin' it."

"I think it does," I say. "It seems the only time when I can get his full attention is when he's locked up. But there are so many things I'd like to talk about and can't because the phones are monitored. And I hate that…canned recording that interrupts our 15-minute phone calls to remind me that I'm talking to someone in a correctional facility, calls that require me to load the phone account weekly. I hate the fact that I know the routine when I visit…all of it makes me so…angry and frustrated!"

"Breathe," says Franklin as he gently rests his hands on my shoulders. "In….out. Breathe, little mama."

I take his advice and take deep breaths as Franklin waits patiently for me to settle down.

"Every day I pray I don't get a call from the prison telling me my son has hanged himself," I say after a while. "I'm so scared that will happen…he's been in solitary confinement."

"For what? Fightin'?"

"No. Remember when I told you he was afraid to take his meds? Well, he thought that if he halved the pills, he wouldn't sleep so hard. One half in the morning, the other half at night if he needed it. The problem with that is…"

"He has extra meds and has to hide 'em," he adeptly responds to finish my sentence.

"Yeah. They did a surprise tossing of the cells and he forgot he had them. They found the pills when they tossed his cell."

"God damn!" swears Franklin.

"I had no idea what had happened to him! I went up there for a visit and they told me I couldn't see him because he was in solitary for a week. When he was finally out, that's when he called and told me."

Franklin sighs and squeezes my shoulders in comfort. We are quiet for a while before Franklin removes his hands to runs a comb through my hair to interrupt our thoughts.

"Is he alright now?"

"He says he is, but I can tell he was traumatized. He's been rubbing his temples as a nervous habit. He has two small bald patches where he rubs. He's gaining weight from all the crappy food. I do what I can to put money on his commissary account because…miracle of miracles…the commissary has some healthy food choices besides Ramen noodles, but the prices are ridiculous I think."

"Ohhhh…is he making mofungo with Ramen and crackers?"

"Yeah! How the hell do you know about all that?"

"I told you one of my sons did some time…not in this state. Dudes get creative in prison when it comes to food," says Franklin.

"You know, the resourcefulness is a little amazing," I agree. "And the bartering for Ramen is almost comical. He hoards his Ramen and Snickers bars just in case he needs to barter for other ingredients to make something."

"If only they cooperated like that outside of prison instead of stealin' and shootin' each other over poison," remarks Franklin.

"If only."

Franklin proceeds to trim my hair as we remain silent. When he's done with the cutting per my wishes, he guides me back to the sinks where Franklin gently leans me back before the strong spray of warm water hits my hair and I close my eyes. He is moving slower than usual today when massaging the shampoo into my hair; his fingers press against my scalp with purpose as he makes small, slow circles starting at hairline and working back to the base of my skull. After he rinses out the shampoo, he uses the same approach with the conditioner. My eyes, first squeezed tight upon the initial water baptism, are now relaxed and the mental turmoil I carried into the salon has settled down. As he guides me back to his chair, I allow a small sigh of satisfaction to escape my lips.

"Thank you," I say quietly after sitting.

"Feelin' a little better?" he asks in a low voice. I nod to confirm.

"This is why your hair is thinnin' out!" chides Franklin. "You were a bundle of nerves the minute you sat down! Hey, I know I got jokes about you women spreadin' yourselves too thin, but I wasn't talkin' about dealin' with a child doin' time. I know some women who's men are servin' time, tryin' to hold things down on the outside. Most of 'em got young children to take care of."

"That's the heartbreaking part of my visits, really," I say. "Families split apart for God knows how long. I mean, I know people need to be held accountable for their actions…I get that. You take someone's life, sell street poison or you steal…go to jail after a trial finds you guilty. But in all of that, the children are going to suffer the most."

"I think about those women who are servin' time," adds Franklin. "Women separated from their kids…got kids either in foster care or with a relative…no money comin' in. Kids gotta talk to their mom on a phone once a day! You can't parent like that. They miss all the important stuff that kids go through. You know what happens to a kid with a parent caught in the system?"

"Nine times out of ten, they wind up repeating the cycle," I respond.

"I heard stories of father *and* son doin' time *at the same time*, get what I'm sayin'? Just tearing down families. And don't forget that a lot of these cases come from plea bargainin'!"

"Like my son's case," I say.

"See? Half the time, there's no trial for lesser cases. The judge offers a plea during pre-trial, and you take it 'cause it's better than facin' the years they were gonna give you. Makes it easy for the lawyers 'cause they don't have to work so hard. Same thing for the judges. Unless it's a murder, drug dealing, guns or money lauderin', they would rather offer a deal than let stuff go to trial so they can pretend they're savin' money and time. If you think about it, you're guilty the minute you step into the courtroom and everythin' else is just background noise!"

"Not to mention the tactics these public defenders use," I add, "which is to ask for continuance after continuance until the case is so old, the court rushes through the case just to get it off the rolls."

"A lot of folks I know took deals. None of their cases went to trial. I don't know the particulars, but I know all of them took deals offered and were told if they tried to fight it, they might get more jail time."

"That's what my son was told this time. He wanted to fight what probation had put on the warrant for the arrest, but his lawyer was like…I'll talk to the prosecutor for less jail time. You feel so helpless…you want to stop the craziness, but if you don't know the law, you're at the whim of a bunch of people who have been at their jobs for so long they don't care if you live or die."

"The system is set up to suck you in and keep you in. And these bonds they set…knowin' full well these poor ass people don't have a nickel to rub together, let alone…what? A thousand for a cash bond?"

"Try $200,000 in the case of my son."

"Say what now? You serious?"

"Very much serious," I say. "To bail him out I would need to put down over $10,000 with a bail bondsman. Even the police station that took him into custody and processed him said the bond was high for a probation violation. And no, the original case didn't involve drugs or guns or murder, and neither did the violations. He didn't even repeat the thing that got him jammed up in the first place. Probation carefully wrote that warrant for the judge to make my son look like a demon that needed to be off the streets. They let a lot of small infractions build up, and then dumped all of them in the warrant and inflated them. And they were minor, like not having his ankle bracelet charged even though it's shitty equipment from a cheap company. Or the time probation showed up at our house and inspected his room to find stuff to violate him over. There was one probation officer who really didn't need to be there, but the lead officer claimed he needed her as backup per policy, knowing full well she hated my son; they constantly clashed."

"What the...? You mean he couldn't find nobody else?"

"Apparently not. She did everything to make my son go off and it worked. Four police officers were called and one of them pulled a gun on him and put him in handcuffs because he wouldn't stay still as they searched his room...*in my home while I wasn't there!* I was in some stupid company training and had my phone on silence and when I came out on break, there were dozens of missed calls. I called him back and he's screaming and crying into the phone over what they did....you hear me? Screaming and crying! I left immediately and went home, which is an hour's drive away."

"Damn, little mama!" says Franklin soothingly. "Pardon my language, but that's some bullshit right there!"

"This probation officer once told my son that even though he had a medical marijuana card for anxiety and PTSD, she would violate him if he popped positive for it on drug tests."

"Oh yeah, I know how probation and parole can jam up a dude. There's no way you can fight 'em on that. Did he ever get transferred to the youth facility?" he asks.

"After some shaming and letter writing to key people, yes. It made things a little easier for him. Decreased his anxiety. Plus, he ran into someone he went to school with…"

"Yeah, nine times out of ten, you'll run into someone you grew up with, from your neighborhood, high school…or somebody who knows the same person you do."

"The last place you expect to run into someone you went to school with. He's been getting gossip from the outside…they gossip like old women, actually! Who's doing what to whom, baby mama drama…you get it all, the news that ain't fit to print!" I finish with a laugh.

"When you got nothin' to do, gossip passes the time!"

"Along with watching talk and game shows."

"All that stuff you talkin' about makes things normal on the inside to people cut off from the world," he says.

"You know, people have this movie version of jail, like everybody is raping or beating the crap out of each other," I say. "If they only knew it's nothing like that. I mean…I can't speak for all prisons, but as far as where my son is, yeah, tempers flare and fights happen, but overall nobody wants to be on lockdown because that means no visits, no commissary deliveries and no rec time, so they calm things down quick. Even in the shower, guys will shower with their boxers on! They don't want anybody looking at their junk."

"I'd do the same thing," he says. "It's a mistake to think nobody's lookin' at what you're packin'. Protect your junk!"

"In all the stuff that my son has told me, one thing I've noticed is that with the exception of a few people, they do try to cooperate with each other, cover each other. And if you know someone they know, it's like…validation…you're legit because you know so-and-so."

"It's no different on the outside if you think about it," says Franklin. "If some strange person starts talkin' to you and they ask you if you know a certain person, don't you start trustin' the person a little? Especially if you're good with the person they mention?"

"I suppose I do trust a little easier, that's true. There's one thing that sorta tugs at my heart, though."

"What's that?"

"Before my son was transferred out of Cheshire, he told me about his cellie there before he went to solitary. He had cancer, an old dude or an 'OG' as they're called. My son said he 'smelled weird' and I had to tell him…"

"It's from the radiation treatment," interrupts Franklin.

"Doesn't that break your heart? You're dying from cancer and you have to suffer in a small cell with a stranger every day and you have no freedom and no privacy. And if you're suddenly in pain, you have to wait until they can take you to the hospital for it. Did you know they treat inmates at the UCONN Health Center, which is practically out in the middle of nowhere?"

"Naw, I didn't. But that makes sense 'cause it's a state hospital, ain't it?" asks Franklin.

"Yup. They go up there in handcuffs and leg shackles. I've seen them."

"And many of them don't have family anymore. Either they're all dead or they got cut out of the family."

"So, they die in prison…alone," I say quietly.

"That's the reality. They weren't thinking about the big C when they did what they did to wind up in jail. And dying alone ain't nothin' new, ya know."

"I know, I know. But I guess this hits closer to home because my son could be in the same position as that OG, body full of cancer and no family there to care about him."

"But he ain't in that position. He's got *you*, momma bear, and your other son. So put that out of your head."

"No, I think I'll keep the thought in my head."

"Why would you do something like that?"

"To remind me that the empathy I feel about it keeps me human. People don't stop and think how important it is to be human, especially when people seem to be at each other's throat constantly."

"Do you really need to think about that OG to feel human, as you call it? To be human, all you need to do is just…be!"

"This is a 'me' thing, Franklin. I always feel the need to stay grounded, remember where I came from, realize that at any moment the same thing can happen to me. I could take someone's life or steal from someone if I'm really desperate and wind up in jail or worse."

"I have nothin' against remembering where you came from," says Franklin. "Keeps a person humble."

"Sometimes I feel the only way to keep being humble is to live in a little bubble. And for a while I lived in a bubble that thought all people played fair. But then you see abuse of power up close and personal, and you see that…soul-stealing abuse affect your child and suddenly you're slicing that bubble open with a machete ready to strike back."

"People need to realize whatever they put forth in this world will come back to them," he says. "You reap what you sow."

"Do you really believe that?"

"Don't you?" asks Franklin. "C'mon, you've seen people get what's comin' to them. Like I said, it may not happen when you want it to, but it do happen eventually. You just ain't around to see it when it do!"

"It doesn't help me right now, though."

"No, I know it don't," Franklin concedes.

"So, I try to do what time can't do for me right now and fight back in my own way. I met those people in probation, like, two days later and basically put them on notice that I see what they're doing."

Chuckling, Franklin asks, "And what they say to that?!"

"It was like the wild, wild west, actually. We stared each other down from opposite sides of the desk while our hands hovered over our hip guns, making silent threats at each other with fake smiles and even faker politeness. I was so disgusted afterwards I went home and took some shots of tequila to calm me down."

After his laughter subsides, Franklin says, "Little mama, all this anger and stress is affectin' your hair. And if it's affectin' your hair, it's definitely affectin' other parts of your body. You a momma bear defendin' her cub, and you should! That system will eat him alive if you let it! But you need to think about what you can control and what you can't. The only thing you can control is bein' there for your cub and tryin' to keep your family together. Those are the important things. The rest, like I said, is background noise."

"Or I could win the lottery and buy my son's way out of the system," I say.

"That would work, too," agrees Franklin. "It's worked before!"

"I was in court one time waiting for my son's case to be called and I've seen how money makes a difference. Have you even done that? See a court hearing?"

"Naw, I've only been on the visitin' in jail side of things, not the court side."

"Well, some of the cases are insane! The stupid stuff people do, like shoplifting or driving drunk or fighting…it makes you wanna yell 'dumbass'! And then there are the cases where people in lockup are brought out in handcuffs and leg shackles…a good portion of them black and Hispanic, and you hear everything they did to earn those shackles. Some of them got multiple cases at different courthouses. And even though some of the stuff they've done deserves punishment, it doesn't stop me from thinking, like, deep down they've gotta be scared about what's facing them."

"That's the thing," says Franklin. "They don't think about what's facin' 'em until they do the dirty stuff. They need to be scared *before* they do it, not after!"

"But when you got money or you come from money, the court responds differently. There was this white kid in front of the judge…I can't remember what he did to wind up there… and the judge is asking him questions about where he goes to school…you know, background stuff. The kid gives him the name of an expensive, private high school in West Hartford. The kid is wearing a suit and tie, with an equally well-dressed lawyer standing beside him. Guess what happened?"

"Judge dismissed the case," guesses Franklin.

"Just about. I think he got community service."

"That sounds about right."

"Here's the flip side of that…if a black person comes in flashing that same type of wealth, a different assumption is made."

"Oh, hell yeah!" agrees Franklin. "First thought is drug dealin'!"

"Or something else illegal. And I hate that people automatically go to that. Why is it inconceivable to a bunch of people who work in a system that's supposed to be blind when it comes to justice that a black person could have access to the same level of wealth as a white person without getting it illegally?"

"Let's be real for a moment, ok?" he says. "The majority of people goin' through the courts on serious charges did what they did 'cause they were tryin' to stack some paper *illegally* and got caught before they could! Street hustlers and wanna be gangstas! Families live in public housing or on Section 8…they survive on food stamps and welfare."

"It's called temporary assistance for needy families now," I quip. "Not welfare."

"Whatever it's called, that's what these people have been on!" he says after slapping my shoulder playfully. "So if a black man….or a woman so I'm not accused of discriminatin', walks in court dressed down and a fancy lawyer beside 'em, it ain't unreasonable to question where that money came from."

"I suppose," I say, considering what he has said. "But questioning the source of that wealth shouldn't be the norm because of skin color. If the justice system is supposed to be blind, you can't take vague clues from a person and make assumptions regardless of how many years you've been doing your job because when you *ass*ume, you make an *ass* out of *you* and *me*! It would be like me assuming you're gay because you're a hairdresser."

"Which I ain't! But people do go there if they don't know me."

"I don't have gaydar…I look for clues. If a guy mentions they have a partner, I'm waiting for that pronoun or name! But even I could see you don't swish!"

"Never swished in my life!" jokes Franklin. "But the stereotype is there…even with you women! A lotta women embarrassed themselves thinkin' I was gay."

"I'm glad I didn't put my foot in my mouth when I first met you!"

"But experience on the job do count for somethin'," says Franklin. "Like, I could tell you were stressed when you sat down in my chair…I always know when you're stressed."

"That's because I'm a regular customer. You developed that six sense about me over time."

"Not just about you. I've been a hairdresser for a long time. A lotta women have sat in my chair, so I've learned to look for signs and just…do what I can to—"

"Franklin," I say, interrupting him, "you're describing emotional intelligence. You can read people, sense their emotions and adjust to them. That's what you have."

"Is that what it's called?"

"It's the best thing to have when you deal with women all day."

"Huh! I'm gonna put you on the phone with my wife and make you repeat that!" jokes Franklin.

"That's what the justice system needs…emotional intelligence."

"What the justice systems *needs* is to hire people *with* emotional intelligence," says Franklin.

"Emotional intelligence with a tablespoon of empathy and a cup of common sense," I add.

Bleeding Red, White and Blue

Every September, Connecticut's Department of Veterans Affairs offers a one-day event called Stand Down, a day for veterans to get what they need, such as free clothes and unmentionables and on-the-spot healthcare to name a few life necessities. This event is held at five different locations across the state, but the one I attend is on the grounds of the state's main Veterans Affairs campus in Rocky Hill. Out of curiosity, and maybe a desire to write a story I can sell, I decide to attend. After winding my way up a slight hill in my silver used compact car, I view a sea of cars neatly parked in a large, grassy field and find a spot. Making my way to the main fairgrounds, busloads of men, in various states of human deterioration, advance upon the grounds of the ten-acre, state-owned property.

There are many tents, each offering a variety of services. The only women present, by my observation, are the wives or daughters of the men they accompany and suddenly, I feel like an oddity in this sea of men. I see acronyms I'm familiar with: USMC, USN, USA, USAF emblazoned on tee-shirts and hats. I also spot sport teams allegiances: NYY and BR (not walking together, of course) and camouflage worn of a puke green and dull, sandy brown colors. Airborne and infantry units were represented as well, "Once a Marine, always a Marine" is on the brim of a ball cap that passed by me. Some men walk on canes of aluminum or wood, others putter around in wheelchairs with the POW logo on the back of the seat. I glance across the field at one of many white tents on the property and a white sign for three tents next to each other is posted over the entryways: Public Defender, Child Support Enforcement and Department of Social Services. Lines of men snake out of the tents; however, the longest line is for the Public Defender's tent. I glance at the men in line to avoid staring too hard and quickly note that the majority of them are black. My eyes are drawn to light-skinned men, caramel-brown men, middle-of–road-brown men, men with skin the color of midnight as I ease by. I spot salt-and-pepper dreadlocks, with nappy coils of hair resting in a ponytail; afros; neat, fade haircut; hair that was once braided waving wildly in the wind. For whatever reason, the men remind me in some way of my Korean War vet father who died in poverty 12 years ago, buried at a national cemetery in Long Island, New York. Chased to his grave early from a hard life wrought with mental illness, homelessness and alcoholism, his reward for serving his country was a simple granite tombstone that encapsulated his life with a name, his branch of service and rank, and his time-in-service on this planet. Without thinking, I mutter to myself,

"There but for the grace of God go I."

Because I start the day late, I arrive at the event near lunch time and my restlessness begins to grow as I roam from tent to tent, not finding anything remotely addressing women who served. Even though I'm not hungry, I decide to take advantage of the free food offered in the cafeteria, which is near the auditorium. As I pass by the platform stage near the side of the auditorium, a live band is playing instrumental blues. I spot a couple of state representatives and constitutional officers congregating near the platform, preparing themselves for their upcoming speeches. I recognize one who I know was a Marine Corp Reserve veteran from the Vietnam-era, so it's no surprise to me that he's there. The state's beauty contest winner stands among them, wearing her crown and banner but conservatively dressed in a cotton, form-fitting turtleneck, dark dress slacks and black heels.

At the entrance to the auditorium there is a long line of men, at least 25 in number, standing patiently for their turn to enter to take advantage of free shoes, undergarments and socks distributed. I overhear a conversation as I pass between two men trying to find the tent that offers free phone cards. Numerous picnic tables are scattered in front, all full of men shooting the shit with their compadres or standing nearby taking in the scene. I overhear the words Girl Scout cookies and I look around frantically before I see the Girl Scouts of America sign posted in front of a dilapidated building next to the auditorium. I smile because there is at least one thing I can take part in: free cookies and I'm hoping the Trefoils and Samoas are plentiful. Passing another white tent that offers free dental exams and foot care, I peek in to see people in white lab coasts, mulling around in the tent waiting for the next patient. I arrive at my destination to snatch the last box of Trefoils, somewhat disappointed to find no Samoas in sight.

I turn around and walk towards the cafeteria and I'm appalled at the poor shape of what I could see of the interior. Absolutely nothing about the building has been updated, not the windows nor the front doors, and the surrounding landscaping is sparse. Another large crowd of older men hover together in front of the entrance, some standing, some sitting on benches. All are smoking cigarettes, eyes squinting to protect eyeballs from the wafting smoke. Their skin is weathered and puckered, and they look older than they probably are. They smoke like the former military men they are, holding their cigarette between the thumb and index finger overhand, or the index finger curled snuggly around the filter. They appear to huddle together as though they are still in trenches or foxholes under the threat of attack. They take deep drags of their cheap cigarette, one puff after another before flicking the butt onto the ground or into an available sand bucket.

As I finally enter the cafeteria, I'm faced with a large American flag hung from the rafters, flanked by flags from the four military branches. Long picnic tables with wood laminate fill the large space, the cacophony of mouths filled with food rises and falls. I follow the crowd to where the food is being served by a line of who I assume are volunteers and staff workers. The food offered is simple: hamburgers, limp hot dogs, water or orange juice, macaroni salad and baked beans. To my utter delight, the dessert offered was every kind of Girl Scout cookie under the Scout's tasty repertoire.

"So that's where the cookies all went," I remark under my breath.

Choosing a dry cheeseburger, chips and only two Samoas (*eat all you want, but eat what you take*), I find an empty seat at a table where a young Hispanic man is sitting with an older Hispanic woman. I offer a brief, polite smile before sitting down with my disposable tray.

"When's your court date?" the woman asks the young man who's wearing a gray, short-sleeved shirt with the word Army in large block letters.

"It's next week."

"You got everything you need? Didja talk to your lawyer?"

"Yeah, yeah," he responds impatiently, sipping his orange juice.

I try to tune out the rest of the conversation to avoid the appearance of eavesdropping. I take a few bites of the dry burger, empty the bag of chips, savor the two Samoas and finish my juice before dumping my refuse and exiting the cafeteria.

Back outside, I stand awkwardly, unsure of what to do or where I should go. Defeated, I decide to head back to my car to leave for the day. A few steps away from the parking field, I spot a tent that is giving away an item that makes me smile. I walk up to the person giving the item away and ask for a particular version of it. Delighted at my response when he's asks me a certain question, he happily gives me the item and I immediately pin it to my jacket.

"Thank you for your service," he says with a smile.

****

"You look happy today! What's up with you?" Franklin asks as I slide into his chair.

"Do I? I don't mean to!"

"What kind of answer is that?"

"The only answer I can give when someone says I look happy," I reply, shrugging.

"Well? Aren't you? You got a little pep in your step today, momma bear. Meet someone special?" asks Franklin.

"What? No! Not at all. I was somewhere that wasn't the best place to pick up any man."

"Prison?"

"No! Why would I—? No, I was at Stand Down yesterday. I went to the one at the main campus for the state's Department of Veterans Affairs. In Rocky Hill…across from a cemetery of all things."

"You know someone who's served?"

"Yeah…me! I was in the Navy for four years."

"You been comin' to me for all these years and you ain't said a word about it! How long were you in for?"

"Four years was all I could give," I reply. "I was a single mom when I was in. Back then, you were deemed government property and having a family is an inconvenience. When it was time to reenlist, the Navy wanted me in Japan with a three-year-old and a *three-month-old*. That's when I parted ways with the Navy. They wouldn't let me stay stateside unless I gave them six years instead of four."

"I would think it'd be excitin' to be in Japan," he says.

"It probably would have," I agree, "but I would've been halfway around the world from my family if something serious happened to me or the boys. You don't know the hassle of getting a military transport for relatives…I wasn't willing to risk it, so I got out."

"I get that. Family comes first. Now, here's the million-dollar question: did you like it?"

A deep, loud sigh comes from my lips as I take time to think about Franklin's question.

"I was young and naïve back then," I begin. "I saw the uniform and I wanted to be a part of all that, but I was naïve about what it all meant and what I'd have to do, the sacrifices, the scrutiny, the sexism, the racism. I threw myself into a world dominated by men and coming from a female-dominated family…I was lost most of the time. I had to develop a male side to who I am; otherwise, I'd be crying all the time."

"Another way to say that is you needed a thicker skin," he says.

"Outnumbered by men at least 100 to 1 depending on the duty station. You can't be weak! There's no crying on the job. There were times when it took everything in me to wait until I got home to let the tears fly. It was just—" I pause for a moment, at a loss for my next set of words.

"There were times when I was so proud to wear the uniform," I continue. "I got a chance to see a battlegroup of ships return to port during Desert Shield/Desert Storm and I'll never forget the roses and mini American flags waving, the excitement and energy. This will sound corny, but I was proud to be an American that day. Not many females can say they were steps away from seeing and hearing an F-15 breaking the sound barrier from the flight deck of a carrier."

"You did that?" Franklin asks with surprise in his voice.

"I did that," I say with a smile. "A lot of amazing stuff. And if I had better guidance, better people who saw my potential, I wouldn't be with you now. But I was harassed for my post-partum weight gain, scrutinized and fired from a department by a known racist and labeled insufficient in performance…I couldn't do it anymore, let alone in Japan. At one time I wanted to be an officer…an ex-boyfriend gave me a box set of Ensign collar devices as a gift."

"Wait…he gave you what?" he asks.

"Collar devices are worn on unforms to signify rank. They let you know who you should solute. Officers have different devices than Enlisted."

"So they have it on the shirt collars and on…what's the things on their shoulders?"

"Shoulder boards…exactly. I got a full set as a gift from an ex to encourage me."

"Sounds like a nice guy! Why is he an ex?"

"Oh, because he lied and cheated on me the entire time and gave away a piece of jewelry I gave him. I think he might have stolen those collar devices because he was only an E-2 and collar devices ain't cheap! But thank you for thanking me for my service because I don't always hear it."

"You can't expect people to know how to respond when they hear you've served."

"Ok, that's fair. But there are certain places where people know to say that kind of thing, but it slips their mind. That mostly happens with men," I say. "It's almost as though people can't process a woman serving the military. We're all over the place if you look! But I've noticed that women who've served don't always toot their own horn about it, same as me. But men? Oh my God…it's like this little boys' club…you can't get them to shut up about it. I saw two guys in a parking lot park opposite each other and one had a

Marine Corp sticker and the other had a veteran Marine Corp license plate. They got out of their cars, started talking about when they served, and then ended it with a 'Ooo-rah!' and I'm like…gimme a break with that.".

"Go figure!" says Franklin.

"But yesterday? I was thanked and I got this! Look!"

I turn around to show him the pin I put on my jacket yesterday, which was a miniature version of a dog tag with ball chain, inscribed with the words all in caps "Navy proudly served."

"Hey, that's cool!" Franklin says as he takes a closer look. "So why were you at…that stand down?"

"You know, that's a good question. I really didn't belong there."

"Why? 'Cause you a woman? You belong anywhere they are."

"Thanks for saying that, Franklin. No…well, I guess part of not feeling like I belong is because I was outnumbered there, seriously! If there was a female vet there, I never saw her!"

"What goes on at this stand down?"

"It's like one large outreach of services…one-stop shopping, you know? If you need health services, socks and stuff…"

"Socks?" asks Franklin.

"Yeah, socks, undies, shoes…dental care—"

"For free?"

"If you're a vet, yes. What broke my heart was the long line of brothahs for the Public Defender's tent. You may see a dash of salt here and there, but it was all pepper brothahs in that line."

"Damn! They even got lawyers there?"

"Child Support Services, too."

"Goddamn! That's good lookin' out!" remarks Franklin.

"It's the least this country could do for the vets, especially since there's a big ass Navy base in Groton! But Franklin, I'm gonna give you permission to do something."

"I'm all ears. What you need?"

"If you *ever* hear me say I'm interested in getting into politics, you have my permission to thump my head like a melon!"

Laughing, Franklin says, "What you fired up about now?"

"Well…last week I went to a town gown meeting with my district representative. That's how I found out about Stand Down—"

"What's a…a town gown?"

"Oh, it's like a town hall meeting. U.S. representatives schedule meetings with people in their district to bring them up to date on stuff that may affect the state. So, for example, say everyone is complaining about getting their IRS refund check, right? The representative might bring a higher up from the IRS to answer questions and what not."

"Do they advertise these meetings anywhere?"

"I'm sure they do, but I have no idea where. I'm on the mailing list. That's how I found out about it."

"What else goes on at these meetings?"

"You get a chance at the mic to ask a question about something federal related. There are a lot of crybabies out there, just so you know."

"And weren't you there to cry too, baby?" jokes Franklin.

"Not on the level of those people. There was this old guy going on and on about the geopolitical history of our relations with China and I'm like…you can go on Reddit for all that! What do you expect this guy to do about it? And the representative is there just smiling and nodding until one of the moderators had to jump in and end the nonsensical rambling. The guy is a regular."

"What happened at that meeting that's got you so fired up?" he asks.

"The original reason I went there flew out the window once I read the flier on the areas of focus and the committees the representative was on. One caught my eye…he's on a committee for Veterans Affairs and I'm like…oh!...I can finally speak my mind on something I know about."

"Did the representative stop you from speakin' or somethin'? You say somethin' wrong?"

"No, nothing like that. I just figured it was the perfect time to tell him about my experience with the VA Healthcare system."

"You have a bad one?"

"Try more than one. But what really aggravates me is the fact that I'm referred out of VA when I need to get a mammogram."

"What's wrong with that? You wanna be in a hospital of mostly dudes while gettin' your lady parts looked at?"

"Yes, I do! I'm a veteran. Discharged honorably. I'm entitled to healthcare from the VA just like any other man and I shouldn't have to go through all the hassle they put me through when I need my annual boob squishing! I have to get a referral from my primary care, then they need to send the order to the radiology office, then I need to call and make the appointment—"

"Wait a minute," says Franklin, "wouldn't you have to do that if you didn't have a VA doctor?"

"Kinda, but—"

"How far is the Vet hospital from here?" asks Franklin.

"It's in West Haven, so about an hour?"

"And the place where you go for your annual—"

"Boob squishing? Maybe 15 minutes."

"Then what the hell is your problem? You'd rather drive an hour instead of 15 minutes? Can't please you women!"

"Will you let me get to the damn point?" I say.

"Ok, what's the damn point?"

"The VA is a hospital! With doctors and nurses who perform surgeries, and they have equipment that includes radiology and ultrasound machines! You know how I know this? Because I've had a long ultrasound wand shoved up my cootchie by a woman with an Eastern European accent in a dim room to photograph my ovaries at the VA! In and out she moves the wand like a sick porno movie and I'm lying there conflicted. Should I feel aroused or violated? And think about this: Why do they have equipment that looks like an 18-inch, ultra-slim dildo? To check prostates! I lucked out over the misery of a man's prostate!"

Franklin stops what he's doing to my hair and doubles over in laughter.

"If they can have equipment for a man's prostate, they can have equipment for, as you call them, lady parts," I conclude when he settles down.

"I got no argument for you! But you still haven't told me what got you heated."

"Right. Almost forgot. Well, I get up to the mic and I speak my peace about mammogram machines at VA hospitals because it's unfair for women to be referred out for those services…it's sexist. You can't say women's contributions to the military are just as valuable as a man's but not include our needs when it comes to health services. We're not the exception anymore; we're part of the rule. I didn't say it like that, but you get the idea.

So, like…two people after me, a black woman gets up to the mic and addresses me and starts talkin' a whole lotta mess. That's what got me fired up!"

"What mess?"

"So, she starts with, 'I want to talk to that young woman over there (points to me) who may not know about the services available…I work at West Haven and the hospital has this and that, so I should check that all out because the VA is doing stuff for women and the VA is addressing the needs through this special center…blah, blah, blah.'"

"I don't get it."

"Ok, let me lay it out for you. Number one, the only thing I said was, in a nutshell, that the VA should have mammogram machines and the VA can do better on that. Number two, I never said the VA wasn't doing anything for female vets; she twisted my words. I even said at the start that the VA had come a long way in treating female vets! I said it! Number three, she made an *assumption* that I didn't know how to find out what services are available to me. If she had approached me one-on-one like a grown up instead of showin' her ass in front of the representative and talking to me like I'm a child, I would've told her I used to work for the VA!"

"Well, you gotta admit, you don't look like your age," says Franklin.

"Wait…wha—? What does that mean?" I ask.

"You don't look your age."

"I never told you my age, so how can you say I don't look like it?" is my next question.

"This is me dodgin' that bullet," quips Franklin.

"Oh, you ain't gettin' out of this! I've never said how old I am. And even if you did know, I challenge this 'not looking your age' thing. Everyone ages differently!"

"So, you're in your sixties like me?" teases Franklin.

"I think not."

"Well, you ain't in your thirties; you know too much old school stuff."

"I see what you're doing here," I say. "Guess what I'm gonna do right now?"

"What that?" asks Franklin.

"I'm gonna plead the Fifth!"

Humanity Has a Chance

We are suffering through three days of 90+ degree temperatures, which is unusual for this time of year. Even worse is the humidity that forces asthma suffers to stay indoors and outdoor people to stay hydrated and keep still. In the old days, even in New York where I'm originally from, we would call this an "Indian summer," but given how offensive that term is today, we now just refer to it as the result of climate change. Luckily, this mini heat wave ends after a torrential rainfall and New England returns to those wonderfully cool autumn days that hint jacket-wearing weather is upon us soon. This change in weather also prompts fanatical leaf peeping adventures and the eating and drinking of pumpkin spice and apple cider everything. But what some New Englanders look forward to the most is the yearly celebration of everything that is quintessentially Yankee, the New England States Exposition, locally known as The Big E.

Held in West Springfield, Massachusetts, The Big E is unique in that every state within New England owns a house on the fairgrounds on a "street" called the Avenue of States. Technically, when you visit a house, you are subject to the laws of the state that owns it should you decide to do something stupid. In each of these houses, you can find food stuff that is unique to the state. For example, if you went to the Maine house, you'll find lobster rolls, baked potatoes stuffed with lobster (or whatever topping you desire) and, believe it or not, Whoopie pies. In Massachusetts, there are apple, cranberry and raspberry treats; local honey (the commonwealth has a regulated apiary program); and, of course, clam chowder. In Vermont, there is, you guessed it, Vermont cheddar cheese and Ben & Jerry's; New Hampshire has the maple syrup; and Rhode Island has clam cakes and chowder. What does Connecticut have? Tobacco from the farms in Windsor and Windsor Locks that have been farmed there for ages. In the past, Pez and Lego held exhibits there. Oddly enough, I've never seen anything nutmeg related.

A state fair isn't complete without carnival rides and games; every type of artery-clogging food you desire, including Fred Flintstone-sized roasted turkey legs and deep fried everything; high-priced but mostly hand-crafted clothes and knickknacks for purchase; and live concerts with well-known musical acts. Daily Mardi gras-like parade floats travel along the Avenue of States, throwing beads at spectators and encouraging *laissez les bon temps rouler.* Special happenings, such as military appreciation day, agriculture and 4-H exhibits and crafts shows can be found on the schedule as well.

Everyone plans carefully when deciding to go because traffic is horrendous in both directions to the fair, especially if a popular act is performing. The parking situation once the grounds are full is cutthroat and pricy as residents and businesses along the main strip to the fairgrounds scramble to sell access to their driveways and parking lots. And even though people complain and threaten not to go because of the hassle, it doesn't stop a million plus people over a 17-day span from sitting in traffic for more than an hour as they inch along to The Big E, including me, who has tickets for this afternoon.

"It's been a long time since you asked for an early appointment on a Saturday!" remarks Franklin as I shimmy into his chair.

"I know! I like to luxuriate in bed and roll out late on the weekends, but not today. I'm taking my sons to The Big E this afternoon. I didn't want to go another week without a relaxer and next weekend I'll be in New York, so here I am, 9 o'clock on a Saturday."

"Your sons don't think it's embarassin' to be with their mom?"

"I was just as surprised as you are that they agreed to go! I'm trying to mend fences between them."

"Brothahs fightin', huh?" he says with a chuckle. "That's normal. I used to fight with my brother all the time."

"And when did you finally stop?"

"In our 50s," says Franklin.

I turn around to face him and pause before I ask, "And how old did you say you are now exactly? Mid-sixties? Late sixties?"

"I didn't say."

"So, basically, you and your brother have been fussin' at each other for most of your adult lives?" I ask.

"With some breaks of gettin' along for a minute…for our mom's sake."

"Which is why I'm dragging both my sons to The Big E," I say, turning back around. "I'm taking them back to when they were small and I didn't have two dimes to rub together and I'd robbed Peter to pay Paul so I could buy tickets and pay for rides and cheap, greasy food. I won't hesitate to remind them of all this when we get there."

"You tryin' to guilt them into being humble, huh?"

"I wouldn't say I'm guilting them into humility…"

"Uh huh…"

"Sometimes we forget how hard we had it when we start earning more money. I'm simply *reminding them* of what we were like as a family when we had next to nothing. We all need those reminders, like when the Pope washes feet of the less fortunate on Easter."

"Are you comparin' yourself to the Pope?" jokes Franklin.

"Absolutely not! You know, I never thought I'd say this, but I wish people paid more attention to Pope Francis."

"Why is that?"

"Because that old man is trying to undo centuries…*centuries* of religious dogma that certain people used to get enormous power and wealth, and that wealth was built on the backs of the poor. He's fighting against people who want to keep things the same and that's a *huge* job for one person."

"I didn't know you were Catholic."

"I'm not. I was christened and raised Episcopalian, which is pretty much the same thing," I say. "Both follow the same rites except Episcopalians don't worship statues or saints. But if you had asked me what I thought about the Catholic church before Pope Francis, I'd tell you it's a broken institution I stay far away from. But I respect Pope Francis. I respect his effort to remind people what the word of God is really all about…forgiveness, love, compassion, empathy.

One day, for whatever reason, maybe part boredom, part curiosity, I was on the Vatican's website reading some of the publications, learning about the Holy Sea. I read the Pope's second…oh, what is it called?…I can't remember what it's formally called, but it's like…a series of recommendations to bishops, priests…and followers on topics regarding marriage…like the church's stance on divorced couples remarrying. The second one he published has a lovely title, *Amoris Laetitia,* which means joy of love. I didn't understand all of it, but I kinda understood the direction the Pope was taking.

I'm not a dyed-in-the-wool Catholic, but to me it seems the popes before Francis made no attempts at inclusiveness or recognizing that the world was changing and the old ways don't work anymore. Let's set aside the abusive priests talk because that's been hacked to death. And the Vatican has been dodgy on the transatlantic slave trade…still. They offered canned responses to the question of responsibility: we condone all forms of slavery."

"I think the young people like him," Franklin murmurs as he applies a pre-treatment to protect my hair from the relaxer creme.

"They do! You don't often see young people excited about a religious figure like that…here in the U.S. I mean. All those young people scrambling for selfies with the Pope. And he agreed to it! I saw all the excitement, this…pope mania and I thought…there's hope."

"Hope for what exactly?" asks Franklin.

"The human race, I guess."

"Whoa!" he exclaims. "How deep are we goin' down that rabbit hole this mornin'?"

I chuckle and say, "Don't worry. I'm not talking about Revelations and the end of days. I mean, well, our world is in chaos right now."

"Agreed," Franklin says as he smooths the relaxer paste.

"We see heartbreaking stuff on the news and social media. Every time you turn around there's been a mass shooting or someone is killed by a police officer or a company's systems has been hacked—"

"Or a child goes missin'…serial killers all over the place…people gettin' conned out of their life's savings—"

"All that stuff and more, right? And then you see the nasty politics, the backstabbing and drama like a badly written nighttime soap opera. The Far Right constantly battling the Far Left for supremacy…it almost sounds like a synopsis for an apocalyptic-type movie."

"Truth is stranger than fiction, they say," he mutters.

"No argument from this corner," I say. "But then I see certain things that people do for each other and if it wasn't for social media I would never be able to actually see it for myself."

"How do you know it's real? Just because it was posted on social media?"

"Whoa, Franklin! Exactly who's going down the rabbit hole this morning?"

Franklin laughs before responding, "My point is, don't rely on social media for proof of hope. Look all around you and if you're payin' attention, you might see it in real time and not on some little screen!"

"I get you. Look for examples of hope everywhere I go, but social media is like…an instant plug in of other feeds that show you there are decent people out there doing amazing stuff."

"I have one problem with all that, but first we need to rinse this relaxer out of your hair. Startin' to tingle a little?"

I confirm it is and we rush to the sink where he neutralizes the relaxer's affect with a special shampoo before applying a deep conditioner. Placing a plastic shower cap on my head, he guides me to a hair dryer, setting the timer for 30 minutes.

As I nonchalantly turn my head to the right, my eyes settle on an unusual scene for a beauty parlor. A grandmotherly woman is sitting on a blanket on the floor in an empty portion of the room, guiding a baby girl of about two years old through what sounds like a children's game app. Each time the toddler got the answer correct, both the game and the older woman would celebrate with the little girl as she squeals in delight and claps her hands. When the little girl got the answer wrong, the older woman would shrug her shoulders in an exaggerated fashion and say, "oh well!" to which the toddler would respond, "oh no!" This scene continues for a while until it's clear the little girl is bored. The woman quickly taps and slides her finger on the tablet screen until the familiar music of a children's show I recognize begins to play and the two settle down to watch.

Though my eyes are still on them, my mind is taken back to a small living room with second-hand furniture in a roach infested, third-floor walk-up in New London. Twenty-three years old and unemployed, I spend my days reading piles of books I borrow from the library where I take my boys somewhere that's free to avoid spending money. As I read, my sons are on a blanket on the floor nearby watching that same children's program, surrounded by action men and Matchbox cars, singing along with the theme song. I smile just as the older woman happens to look up at me; she smiles back.

Franklin comes for me right before the dryer shuts off and leads me back to the sink to rinse out the conditioner. Towel drying my hair, he brings me back to his chair.

"So, what's your problem," I ask.

"Huh?"

"You said before you had a problem with me plugging in to social media to find examples of hope."

"Hold on a sec, I lost my train of thought on that one…" Franklin trails off. A beat later, he says,

"Yeah, here's my problem, and it goes back to whether what you think you're seein' really happened. Have you ever thought about how convenient it was that someone was recordin' right at the moment that nice thing happened? Like the fast food worker who's surprised by a new car from his co-workers 'cause he's been walkin'…like, eight miles to work for 16 years."

"Franklin!" I exclaim as I control my laughter.

"That dude is probably makin' $7.50 an hour fryin' chicken fingers and now he's gotta pay taxes, insurance, registration. If I were him, I'd sell it, pay some bills and get a damn scooter."

"Franklin!" I say, still attempting to control my laughter.

"I'm serious! Did they really do that guy a favor by poolin' their money for a car he can't afford? They shoulda just given him the money!"

"You're missing the point of the gesture—"

"And if you're gonna do something nice for someone," interrupts Franklin, "why do you have to record it all? So you can post it and say, 'Look at what we did? See how nice we are?' Stranger walks up to you in front of a supermarket with a camera and gives you money out of the blue…of course you're gonna cry on camera! You gotta work that camera like a pole 'cause you just got $500 in cash. And how stupid are those people to take that money on camera? Knock, knock! It's the IRS lookin' for you and the guy that gave you that money!"

"I forgot how sharp you are in the morning," I say, wiping away laughter tears.

Out of the store front window, I see a silver SUV pull up to the front door. A woman of about my age rushes to the passenger side door and opens it to show a frail older woman with glasses and wearing a colorful windbreaker. They talk for a moment before the younger woman disappears towards the rear of the SUV out of sight. She returns pushing a folded wheelchair; she opens it and then gently assists the older woman out of the passenger seat and into the wheelchair, handing her a purse and a collapsible walking cane. Franklin, spotting them, moves quickly to the door and holds it open for the two women.

"How you doin', Miss Emma?" is how Nona, the salon owner, greets the woman in the wheelchair.

"I'm well, I'm well. How about yourself?"

"Ma'am, the Lord is treatin' me well," says Nona. Addressing the younger woman, she says, "Hey, Terry, good to see you!"

"Good to see you, too," replies Terry.

"Did you know today is my birthday?" asks Miss Emma.

Nona, stifling a smile and giving Terry a knowing look, says, "I think Terry said something to me. And how old are you today?"

"Ninety-three!"

Everyone, including me, starts to clap as Miss Emma smiles and nods.

"Well, happy birthday, Miss Emma!" gushes Nona. "May God bless you and keep you today! And what can I do for the birthday girl?"

"I need my hair done for my birthday party this afternoon. All my family is gonna be there and I wanna look good."

"Oh, yes, ma'am!" replies Nona. "You think you gonna be able to get in my chair? Franklin can help."

Miss Emma looks up at the tall, thin, younger-looking Franklin who is standing with his slightly muscular arms folded across his chest, a grin on his face. She flashes a denture filled smile and says, "Oh, that would be nice! Will you help me?"

"Yes, ma'am, I can do that," he replies.

Terry wheels Miss Emma as close as possible to Nona's salon chair. Nona cues Franklin, who then gently lifts Miss Emma out of the wheelchair and into the salon chair.

"Oh, thank you!" says Miss Emma, still smiling.

"You're welcome and happy birthday! If you need my help again, you let me know, ok, birthday girl?"

Miss Emma giggles and says, "I will. Thank you."

Terry, who I later learn is Miss Emma's great niece, withdraws the now empty chair, folds it and puts it out of the way. She tells Nona she's going to park her SUV and leaves. Franklin comes back to me and wets my hair with a spray bottle to continue his work trimming my hair.

"You'll flirt with anyone, won't you?" I joke.

"Do you see her complainin'? Besides, I have a way with all women! Don't matter how old they are!"

"I think you made Miss Emma's day," I say as I look over at her chatting away with Nona.

"It don't take much to make someone's day."

We are quiet for a moment before I break the silence with, "You're right."

"Flirtin' for a cause! There's nothin' wrong with that!"

"No, I mean about the other thing. About hope for the human race all around you."

Franklin playfully taps me on the shoulder and says, "Now you get it. And not a camera in sight."